LAST SUMMER IN LOUISBOURG

CLAIRE MOWAT

NIMBUS
PUBLISHING

Nimbus Publishing Limited
3731 Mackintosh St, Halifax, NS B3K 5A5
(902) 455-4286 nimbus.ca

Printed and bound in Canada

Previously published by Key Porter, ISBN-13: 9781550139419

Design: Heather Bryan

*This novel is a work of fiction. Names, characters, places, and incidents are either
the product of the author's imagination or are used fictitiously.*

Library and Archives Canada Cataloguing in Publication
    Mowat, Claire
    Last summer in Louisbourg / Claire Mowat.
    Issued also in electronic format.
    ISBN 978-1-55109-894-4

I. Title.
PS8576.O985L37 2012   jC813'.54   C2011-907633-0

Canadä Canada Council / Le Conseil des Arts   NOVA SCOTIA
for the Arts / du Canada   Communities, Culture and Heritage

Nimbus Publishing acknowledges the financial support for its publishing
activities from the Government of Canada through the Canada Book
Fund (CBF) and the Canada Council for the Arts, and from the
Province of Nova Scotia through the Department of Communities,
Culture, and Heritage.

MIX
Paper from
responsible sources
FSC® C016245

For Justin Mowat
∞ CM

CHAPTER ONE ❖

"I won!" Andrea shrieked the instant she hung up the phone. "I won! I won!" Overjoyed, she galloped down the stairs in her worn-out jeans and sweatshirt and bare feet. She didn't bother to comb her hair. There actually were occasions when it didn't matter what you looked like, and this was one of them.

"What is going on?" her mother called from the small room beside the kitchen, where she worked at her desk most evenings. She was a teacher, and she had lessons to prepare and papers to mark.

"Mom! You're never going to believe this." Andrea panted as she rushed into the room.

"Calm down. Believe what, sweetie?"

"I won!"

"Won what?"

"That contest. Remember? I wrote a history essay and my teacher, Mrs. Greenberg, entered it in that contest for students."

"And you won?" her mother asked incredulously.

"Yes, I did."

"Fantastic!" her mother cried, and hugged her daughter. "To tell the truth, I'd forgotten all about that contest."

"Me too. Well, almost. Actually, I'm not the only winner. There's one from each province and territory. I won the Ontario prize."

"Wait till we tell Brad," exclaimed her mother joyfully. "He'll be so proud of you."

Brad was down in the basement installing a workshop, a place where he could fiddle around with his power tools. He loved fixing things. Brad was Andrea's stepfather. He was okay, but he could never replace her real father, who had died when Andrea was a little girl. Her mother had married Brad a year and a half earlier and that had abruptly changed their lives. When Andrea and her mother lived in an apartment by themselves, life had been a lot simpler. She didn't have to share her mother with anyone. It was nice that Brad could fix faulty toasters and broken porch railings. If only he wasn't always barging into their lives with his own complicated plans.

Brad emerged from the basement with wood shavings clinging to his T-shirt and dust coating his glasses. He grinned when he heard the news. "Terrific, kiddo! Naturally we knew all along you were going to win... didn't we, honey?" He winked at Andrea's mother.

"You bet," she agreed. "So, what's the prize?"

"You'll never guess."

"Now let me see," pondered Brad. "What about a gilt-edged, leather-bound edition of *The Life of Sir John A. Macdonald*?"

"Yuck," said Andrea. "Better than that."

"I thought you liked Sir John A. Macdonald. I thought he was one of your heroes," said her mother.

"Sort of."

"Because you share a birthday, right?"

Andrea Baxter and Canada's first prime minister had both been born on January the eleventh—about a century and a half apart. It was a rotten time of the year to have a birthday, Andrea had often complained. Always freezing cold, it was too soon after Christmas and New Year's for anyone to think about presents and parties again. The only good thing was that the principal of Willow Drive School always called an assembly to celebrate Sir John A.'s birthday and inevitably Andrea got some spin-off attention since it was her birthday too. She kept hoping the Canadian government would declare the day a national holiday, but so far that hadn't happened.

"I didn't write about Sir John A. Macdonald. I wrote about...don't you remember?"

Her mother thought for a moment. "Ah, yes, the Battle of the Plains of Abraham. I read it over before you submitted it. It was first-rate."

"So the prize has to be a trip to the Plains of Abraham, right?" Brad queried.

"You're close. It's a trip. But even better than that."

"Better? How?" asked her mother.

"Farther away."

"Farther away is better, is it?"

"I don't mean that. It's just that I always wanted to visit this place. There were pictures of it in a book at school. You see, the prize for each winner is a summer job with Parks Canada. The man who phoned to tell me I won asked me if I had a preference—like, did I want to see the Rocky Mountains or Quebec or Saskatchewan or whatever. So I told him I was born on the East Coast and I liked it there. He asked me if I spoke any French, and I told him I'd been in an immersion class for years and it was no problem. So he suggested the Fortress of Louisbourg on Cape Breton Island. And I said that would be awesome!"

"Louisbourg?" repeated her mother, looking startled. "Louisbourg!"

"Right, Mom. They have an incredible fortress there. It's an entire town that's been rebuilt just like the old days. It's something like Upper Canada Village, only bigger, and this one is French, and you get to wear old-fashioned clothes if you work there. Oh, I can hardly wait!" Andrea cried.

"You're going to spend an entire summer in… Louisbourg." There was no enthusiasm in her mother's voice. "It's…it's…so far away."

"Mu-um," grumbled Andrea, in the tone of voice she always used when she was fed up. "It isn't as far away as Newfoundland, and I've been there lots of times visiting our relatives."

"You don't have any aunts or uncles or cousins in Cape Breton, though, and Newfoundland and Cape Breton Island are not all that close together. I'm just concerned you might be…well, lonely if you go."

"*If* I go. What do you mean, 'if'? I already told them that I would take the job, that I really, really wanted to be there," Andrea protested.

"I'd certainly like more details about it," her mother insisted. "What if you run into difficulties? What if there are problems?"

"Mu-um! For Pete's sake! There won't be any problems. They said they'd arrange for a place for me to stay and everything. This is a job in a million. I absolutely have to go," Andrea pleaded.

"You earned it, kiddo, you really did." Brad chimed in. His wife shot him a dark look that said he had better keep out of this.

Andrea was surprised—and pleased—that he had spoken up on her behalf. Sometimes, she grudgingly acknowledged, Brad could be almost human, and she did have to admit that he had managed to make her mother a happier person than she had been. But he was always trying to change things. It had been his idea that they move out of their perfectly nice apartment in the Toronto suburb of Willowdale. Now they lived in a brick house in Trillium Woods, a far-too-small town beyond the boundary of Metropolitan Toronto. Out there everything seemed so far away—the mall, the new school she attended, the fitness centre where she swam, and, of course, Suzy, her best friend, whom she had had to leave behind in Willowdale. Now when she wanted to go anywhere she had to get her mom or Brad to drive her to the train station. As far as she could judge, nothing even vaguely interesting ever happened in Trillium Woods. Andrea was dying to get out of the place.

"Andrea," said her mother in the ultra-serious tone of voice she reserved for heavy discussions. "I know you deserve this prize. But it is a long way from home and you are only fifteen years old, and I need to know a few things before you go there all by yourself. I'll give Mrs. Greenberg a call. And I'd like to know the name of whoever is in charge of things at Parks Canada. Also, I want you to think it over for a few days. It might turn out you don't really want to go."

"*Mu-um*! How can you even think that? Of course I want to go. Where else am I going to find a summer job, anyway?" Andrea groaned. What was all the fuss about? Last year her mother had gone off to Africa to teach school for six months, sending Andrea to Newfoundland to stay with her aunt and uncle. Her mother had always been proud of her own adventurous spirit. She said it ran in the family, and Andrea had it too. Now, all of a sudden, she was acting as if Andrea was a baby who couldn't look after herself.

"It's getting late and there's school tomorrow," her mother declared flatly, but added in her normal, kindly voice, "I know you're very excited, sweetheart, and truly it is wonderful news that you won this prize. You probably don't feel like sleeping but do try. I imagine tomorrow will turn out to be a very exciting day at school for you."

"Oh, Mom," Andrea grumbled, even as she gave her mother a goodnight hug and headed upstairs to her room.

"This proves conclusively, as we should already know, that war is a terrible thing. This battle should never, never have been fought. Nobody won. In the long run it didn't prove very much. There was plenty of space for everyone, as things turned out. General Wolfe and General Montcalm both died horrible deaths"—here Andrea paused dramatically as she emphasized the words "horrible deaths"— *"and so did many fine young soldiers. But worse than that,"* she continued passionately, *"it meant that there would be a legacy of bad will between the French and the English in Canada for many, many years to come. If that dreadful battle had never occurred, then we could have worked out our differences and lived together more harmoniously.*

"In conclusion, I would like to say that war and battles are a waste of lives, time, and money. People should always sit down together and talk it over and work things out. That way the world would be a better place.

"Thank you very much."

Andrea sat down. Everyone in the assembly room clapped as she finished reading her prizewinning essay. She could feel her face turning the same shade of Desert Rose as her nail polish. She fidgeted in her chair and focused on the braided silver ring on her finger.

When the applause died down, Mrs. Greenberg, the teacher who had submitted her essay to the contest, stood up. She told the audience how proud the school was that one of their students had won this important prize. She announced that Andrea Baxter would be leaving in June to spend the summer working at the Fortress of Louisbourg on Cape Breton Island, Nova Scotia.

There was a moan of envy from her classmates. They were all hoping to get summer jobs—anywhere.

Mrs. Greenberg went on to remind the students that there were a lot of books in the library about Canadian history. There would be another contest next year. It would be a good idea to begin preparing for it right away, as Andrea obviously had.

"Remember, it wasn't a matter of mere luck that Andrea won this contest. It was due to the effort she brought to the task," Mrs. Greenberg concluded.

Andrea squirmed and stared into the middle distance. She knew what the other kids would think of that. To her relief the bell rang. Assembly was over. Everyone got to their feet and shuffled noisily out of the auditorium.

CHAPTER TWO ❖

"Andrea, you can still change your mind. You don't have to go if you don't want to."

"Mom. Honestly. You know how I feel." Her mother sighed. "I'd feel much better about it if I could come with you."

The two of them were having breakfast in the sunny kitchen. Andrea couldn't finish eating hers, she was so excited. This was the day she was leaving for Cape Breton Island.

"I'm going to be perfectly okay. I like travelling, remember?" She couldn't figure out why her mother had turned into such a worry-wart all of a sudden. "I get on the train and then we take off. It's like an airplane, only it stays on the ground."

"But you have to change trains in Montreal and wait an hour or more for the train to the Maritimes. Stay in the station and don't talk to any strangers."

"I never do," Andrea reminded her fretful mother. "I've got a book I'm supposed to read, *A Guide to the Fortress of Louisbourg*. When that's finished, I've got my stereo with two new tapes," she said, patting her bulging duffle bag.

"I wish I hadn't agreed to do a summer course," her mother lamented. Having spent six months teaching in West Africa, she and Brad had agreed to instruct a number of other teachers who were going to work overseas.

"Aw, Mom, you'll enjoy it. You always do."

"I'll miss you."

It was embarrassing the way her mother got sentimental at times like this. Andrea would make plans to go somewhere and then, when it was time to leave, you'd think it was the end of the world.

"I'm coming back. It's only a summer job," she said reassuringly, giving her mother a big farewell hug.

Her mother drove her to Guildwood station, where the train to Montreal made a brief stop. Andrea climbed aboard quickly, gave a final wave goodbye, then headed down the aisle looking for a seat. She wanted to sit beside the window, but the coach was almost full. She finally spotted a window seat but had to climb over a long-legged, sloppily dressed man who appeared to be asleep. He stirred and grunted and then ignored her as she brushed past him and sat down.

The train gathered speed and Andrea stared out the window while the hot, leafy suburbs of Toronto rolled by. The houses thinned out and they passed a golf course and then were in wooded countryside. Here and there she caught a glimpse of the pale water of Lake Ontario under a hazy, humid sky. She began to daydream about the ocean, and about Louisbourg. What was it going to be like, really?

Her reverie was interrupted by the conductor striding along the aisle asking to see everyone's tickets. Andrea dug hers out of the pocket of her duffle bag and handed it to him.

"Truro," muttered the conductor. "Truro. So you're going all the way to Truro, Nova Scotia," he said as he handed her the remainder of her multi-paged ticket.

"I'm going to Sydney," Andrea corrected.

"So you are. But Truro is where you get off the train and catch the bus for Sydney. You have a separate ticket for that. See, there it is." He pointed it out.

After a while another man came along the aisle with a trolley containing food and beverages. Andrea ordered a tuna sandwich and some ginger ale. The fellow beside her woke up and ordered some sandwiches too.

"Jeez. Railway food!" he grumbled as the train was whizzing past a town named Trenton Junction. Andrea thought the sandwich didn't taste too bad, but this grumpy, unshaven guy in the faded grey sweatshirt and stained blue jeans continued to complain, even as he wolfed down the sandwiches.

"So, where you off to?" he asked Andrea when he had finished.

"Louisbourg. That's on Cape Breton Island. I'm going to Sydney first. Somebody's meeting me there," she added, just so he wouldn't think she was alone in the world.

"Huh, Sydney. Armpit of the earth. Me, I'm headin'
for Cape Breton too. Glace Bay. Had it up to here with
Upper Canada," he complained.

Andrea wasn't sure if he was referring to Upper
Canada Village or Upper Canada College, but decided
not to ask. He seemed to be in a bad mood.

"I've got a summer job in Louisbourg," she offered,
and then wondered if she should have told him that
much about herself.

"One of the lucky ones, are ya?"

"Guess so."

"That's your home, Louisbourg?"

"No, I live…near Toronto."

"And you got a job in Louisbourg? You takin' a job
away from some Maritimer? Holy shit!"

"Actually, I'm from the East Coast originally. I was
born in Newfoundland," Andrea shot back.

"Hah, a goofy Newfie," he snorted.

Andrea felt a rush of anger. "If you must know, the
reason I got this job was because I won a contest, an
essay contest about Canadian history. The prize was a
summer job with Parks Canada," she told him tartly. That
should put him in his place.

"So you're a smart ass too!" he guffawed.

"And you're a stupid jerk," she thought, but didn't say
it.

Her mother had been right, Andrea thought. She
should not talk to strangers. Who wanted to listen to

this guy's insults? She vowed she wouldn't speak another word to him. She hauled her book out of her bag and began to read it as the train was pulling into the station at Belleville. She concentrated on the book for the rest of the afternoon until the train reached Montreal.

The aim of the Fortress of Louisbourg is to portray a moment in time: the summer of 1744 when the fortress was nearly complete and the town had yet to suffer bombardment and conquest. Archaeologists have excavated the remains of the original buildings. The historical staff has assembled evidence for every aspect of Louisbourg life, the buildings and their uses, the goods that filled them, the people who lived here, the society and economy that shaped them.

The Fortress of Louisbourg continues to train and employ workers in building skills once thought extinct, in craft industries, even in eighteenth-century tailoring and deportment. Soldiers and families in period dress renew the activities of Louisbourg's people."

There was a different atmosphere on board the overnight train to the Maritimes, and Andrea saw no more of her former seat mate. Her ticket entitled her to a lower berth. A friendly porter explained how he would turn her seat into a bed while she was eating dinner. In the dining car another cordial man, who appeared to be in charge of things, ushered her to a table where three women were already seated.

"Hello there," one of them said, reaching for a dinner roll and a pat of butter. Andrea only nodded. She wasn't interested in getting involved in another conversation with strangers. For quite a while she simply listened to them. They all knew one another, that was certain, and they were very chummy with two men sitting at the table across the aisle. All three women wore a lot of eye makeup and huge, dangling earrings.

"They're our brothers," one of them remarked in an aside to Andrea as the conversation bounced back and forth between the two tables. "Bill and Gord."

"And we're sisters," added another one. So this was an entire family of brothers and sisters all going somewhere together. Andrea wondered where they were going, and finally got up her courage to ask.

"Cornerbrook, Newfoundland," they replied. "That's where we belong, originally, but none of us lives there now. I live in Toronto. My sister here lives in Vancouver. This other one lives in Atlanta. Bill lives in Sudbury and Gord lives in Brantford."

"Is this a family reunion or something?"

"No, dear, we're going home to bury our father," explained the lady from Atlanta solemnly.

"Oh, I'm sorry," offered Andrea, feeling embarrassed.

"Don't you fret, girl," said the Vancouver sister. "You couldn't have known that. And where are you off to, all by yourself?"

Andrea decided she could tell them where she was going. She also told them that she, too, came from Newfoundland, that her parents had brought her to

Toronto as a small child but she had returned to visit Newfoundland several times.

After that her companions treated her like one of their own, and the meal they had together became great fun. It wasn't until the main course was being served that Andrea realized Gord was blind. His brother helped him out by reading the menu or placing his hand on his coffee cup or cutting his steak for him. Apart from that, Gord chatted and joked with his sisters and managed to eat his dinner without any problems.

"And who is the young lady at the other table talking with my sisters?" Gord asked, picking up on the sound of Andrea's voice.

"My name is Andrea. Andrea Baxter," she replied a little shyly, not knowing precisely how to handle this situation.

"I hope you have a good journey, Andrea," he said, looking in her direction but not seeing her. "And remember, us Newfs have to stick together!"

When the meal ended, Andrea paid her bill and got up to return to her reserved seat. "Now, my dear, if you get lonesome, we're going to have a little game of cards back there in the club car. You come and join us, why don't you?" invited the sister who lived in Toronto.

"Um…thanks a lot, but I really ought to go to bed. I have a lower berth," Andrea explained, then wondered if she should have mentioned where she was going to sleep. Who were you supposed to trust? These people were so nice…but…

"Well, girl, if you change your mind…"

"Thank you."

Andrea returned to her place in car number 1603 to find the double seat had been transformed into a bed totally enclosed by heavy, dark green curtains. Inside, it was as private as a tree-house and as dark as a coalmine. Andrea located the switch and turned on the light. The porter had lowered the window blind, but, after putting on her pyjamas, she raised it, then switched out the light. For a long time she stared out the window as the darkening countryside sped by. Here and there she could see lights from lonely looking farmhouses. Every so often the train whizzed through a small Quebec village or town. At highway crossings she could hear the muffled ding-ding-ding-ding-ding-ding of the warning signal. How many times had she been in her mother's car when they had stopped at a level crossing to wait for a train to pass by? It was fascinating to be inside the train at night, in one's own private space, looking out at the world. Andrea wasn't the least bit sleepy. She decided to unpack her stereo. What better place and time to listen to her new tapes?

The melancholy voice of her favourite singer seemed to suit the black landscape. For a long time the train travelled through a forest with no lights to be seen anywhere. After a while they passed into another farming region. Then Andrea began to see large buildings— warehouses and factories—and dimly lit streets and alleys with wires overhead. All the signs were in French. The train slowed and at ten o'clock squealed to a full stop.

Beyond the railway tracks Andrea noticed a body of shimmering water. There, on the other side of the wide St. Lawrence River, stood an illuminated Quebec City. Windows in the tall buildings glittered against a navy blue sky. She could see the turreted roof of the Chateau Frontenac dominating the skyline of the lower town. It looked like a huge fairy castle from one of her childhood story books.

She yanked off her stereo earpiece as she suddenly realized where she was. "That's it! That's where the battle took place, up there above the old city! I can see the Plains of Abraham where Wolfe and Montcalm fought!"

It was an incredible moment—but there was no one with whom to share it. She felt sad and alone. She wished her best friend, Suzy, was with her. Or even her teacher, Mrs. Greenberg. For a moment she considered getting dressed and walking back to the mysterious club car, wherever that was, and joining the chummy family from Cornerbrook. She envied them, travelling together and having fun, even if they were going to a funeral. The trouble was she didn't want to play cards. She wasn't very good at it. If she interrupted their game to tell them she had just seen the Plains of Abraham, where the famous battle was fought, what would they say? "So what?" Would they laugh at her? They might even call her a smart ass.

Ten minutes later there was a hissing sound, followed by a cloud of steam rising outside the window of her lower berth. As the train dragged its great weight into motion Andrea caught the name on the station: LÉVIS. She pressed her nose against the window and watched the enchanted city across the river disappear from view. She put her stereo away, pulled the crisp, white sheet and the beige wool blanket around her shoulders, and snuggled down. She had stopped feeling lonely. The rhythmic beat of the train wheels on the tracks lulled her to sleep. Tomorrow morning she would wake up somewhere else.

CHAPTER THREE ❧

"You must be Andrea Baxter," declared the smiling young woman who approached her at the Sydney bus station. "You look just the way I pictured you from your letter. Isn't that amazing? I'm Jackie Cormier. Welcome to Cape Breton!"

Andrea managed a weak smile, more of relief than joy. She was enormously grateful that someone was actually here to meet her, as had been promised. For the final hour of the long bus trip from Truro she had worried about what she would do if no one showed up. What if she found herself all alone in Sydney, Nova Scotia, late at night in a place she had never been before? She was feeling disoriented under the glaring lights amid a crowd of strangers. It had been a long journey, twenty-five hours on the train and another five on the bus.

Jackie helped Andrea carry her luggage out to the parking lot, where she stowed it in the back seat of her bright blue Pontiac Firefly. Andrea gradually began to relax. From the outset Jackie seemed like the sort of person you could trust, a down-to-earth woman who wore a sporty red raincoat and tiny gold earrings in her pierced ears. She was slender, and was the same height as Andrea, five feet five. Her hair was a nondescript shade of brown and had been cut dramatically short, a style that suited her heart-shaped face and her mirthful blue eyes.

Fine, silvery rain began to fall as Jackie drove out of the city towards Louisbourg, half an hour away. She was a cheerful, talkative person and during the journey Andrea learned that Jackie was a public relations officer at the fortress. She worked there all year round. Apparently there was a lot of work to do, even when the place was closed to the public for the winter.

Jackie had always lived in the present-day town of Louisbourg, which was near the fortress. She was twenty-six years old and married to Steve, a helicopter pilot, who was away in Labrador all summer. She was the mother of a little boy named Kenzie, who had just turned five.

By the time they pulled up outside the Northeast Bed and Breakfast in Louisbourg, Andrea felt a lot more at ease. Jackie was going to be her supervisor for the next two and a half months and, barring some unforeseen quirk in Jackie's personality, she was sure they would get along.

Andrea got out of the car and stretched, then looked around at the town of Louisbourg—as much of it as she could see under the street lights. There was a gift shop across the street, a gas station next to that, and a motel farther along. None of it looked the least bit interesting.

"I live around the corner," said Jackie. "See that white house up the hill there? That's mine," she pointed.

"So where's the fortress?" Andrea asked.

"Over there, beyond the town, way across the harbour," Jackie gestured. "I'm sure you must be dying to see it, and you will—tomorrow. Right now you need to get settled in your new home and meet your roommate."

Andrea followed Jackie in the front door of the Northeast Bed and Breakfast. It was a tall, frame house, painted dark green with white trim. It was very quiet inside, as if everyone had gone to bed.

"This is my Aunt Roberta's home. She'll be asleep by now. She only rents out the two rooms—yours and one other, so even at the height of the tourist season there won't be too much of a line-up for the bathroom," Jackie explained as they climbed the creaky stairs. At the end of a dark hallway was a partly open door and a lighted room beyond. Jackie tapped and they walked in.

"Justine, here's your roommate, Andrea Baxter. Andrea, this is Justine Marchand," Jackie introduced them.

Justine was tall, with shoulder-length dark hair and dark brown eyes. She was dressed in pyjamas with a pattern of zebras all over them.

"Oh, I am so glad you got here. I've been waiting

and waiting and waiting!" she exclaimed with as much enthusiasm as if she'd been waiting for the Queen.

"Have you been here a long time?" asked Andrea, tossing her duffle bag on the floor.

"Ever since Sunday. But now I won't have to sleep in this room all by myself. You want to know something? I've never slept in a room alone before, never ever, until I came here."

Andrea hardly knew how to reply. She had always had a room to herself. "You must have a sister," she said.

"I've got two sisters. And a brother. Sylvie is my twin sister. Then there's my little sister, Holly. She's only ten. My brother, Marc, is seventeen. Sylvie and I've always, always shared a room and for a long time Holly was in with us too, but then my dad built an upstairs on our house and Marc moved his room up there and Holly moved into Marc's room. We have bunks, Sylvie and I," Justine rambled on, apparently in an enormous hurry to tell Andrea all the details of her life.

"So, does your twin sister look just like you?"

"No way. We're not identical. We're fraternal twins. Sylvie is, oh, she has reddish sort of hair, only hers is really long."

"I'm letting mine grow," said Andrea, trying to get a word in.

"And she has greenish-grey eyes. And she's not as tall as I am. And she's fat. At least, I tell her she's fat. I bet she weighs eight or nine pounds more than I do," continued Justine with a grin. "I'll guarantee she doesn't like it when you call her fat! She gets so mad. She throws pillows at me sometimes. Mom gets mad at both of us when the feathers fly around. What about you, Andrea? How many brothers and sisters have you got?"

"None. I'm an only child," Andrea admitted defensively. She often wished she did have a sister or a brother.

"Oh," was Justine's only comment.

"I am an only child too, Andrea. I know what it's like," said Jackie kindly.

"I've got some cousins, in Newfoundland," Andrea said, trying to make her family situation sound less bleak. "I go there to visit them. Quite often."

"I've got a lot of cousins too. Really a lot. They're nearly all in Cape Breton, except for four who moved to Alberta."

"Now then," Jackie interrupted firmly. "I'm sure you two have a lot to talk about, but it's very late. There's going to be plenty of time to get acquainted tomorrow. You'll need your sleep. We get up early around here, don't we, Justine?"

"Tell me about it," groaned Justine, climbing into her bed. There were twin beds and both had quilts. Justine had a green one with a design of interlocking circles. Andrea's bed had a yellow one with a design of tulips and leaves.

When the lights were out and the girls were supposed to be asleep, Justine leaned over and whispered, "Andrea, are you awake?"

"Yes."

"Do you know what we could do tomorrow?"

"What?"

"We can go down the road and get some pop and chips. I know a place. We can walk there. It only takes about five minutes. Wanna go?"

"I guess so," replied Andrea cautiously. "But I want to see the fortress tomorrow."

"Oh, did you never see it?"

"How could I? I've never been here before."

"Well, I saw it plenty of times. Even before I came to work here."

"Where do you live?"

"River Bourgeois."

Andrea had never heard of the place, but she didn't want to sound stupid by asking too many questions. "I'm from Toronto—well, close to Toronto—and that's a long way from here."

"Don't worry. You'll see the fortress all right. You'll get sick of it before you know it. What I meant was we could go for some pop and stuff after we get off work, around five, okay?"

"Sure. Sounds neat," replied Andrea.

"Okay. G'night," said Justine.

Andrea was exhausted, but she had trouble falling

asleep right away. So much had happened in a short time. Here she was in a strange room in an unfamiliar town with this bubbly roommate who was apparently more interested in going somewhere for a snack than she was in the Fortress of Louisbourg. Andrea hoped they would get along, but at that moment she wasn't exactly sure.

CHAPTER FOUR ❖

Justine turned out to be one of those people who could bounce out of bed in the morning with the energy of a wind-up toy. Andrea wasn't like that. She usually woke sluggishly, wishing she could sleep for another hour. Today she was glad her roommate was so alert. Andrea had a hundred questions. Where did they get their breakfast? How would they find their way to the fortress? She didn't even know what time they were supposed to start work.

They dressed, then Andrea followed Justine down the stairs to the dining room, where the ingredients for breakfast were spread out on a large table. There was no one else in the room. A few minutes later Roberta MacNeil cautiously opened the kitchen door and peered in. She had frizzy grey hair and wore a flowery apron around her ample waist.

"Good morning," said Andrea, her mouth full of toast.

"So you're the new girl, are you?"

"Yes, I am," Andrea answered, thinking that was a pretty dumb question. What would Mrs. MacNeil have done if she had replied that she'd been here for weeks?

Mrs. MacNeil had nothing else to say. She returned to the kitchen, leaving the girls by themselves.

"Never mind her," whispered Justine. "She keeps to herself a lot."

Maybe just as well, thought Andrea.

After breakfast they headed towards the fortress on foot. "You can't possibly get lost in Louisbourg," Justine reassured her. "There's only the main street and then it becomes the highway and then it ends at the fortress."

"How far is it?" Andrea wanted to know. She couldn't see any trace of the place. By then they had reached the edge of the town and there were no more houses or stores. The road ahead led through a forest of stunted spruce trees.

"Couple of miles. Couple of kilometres maybe. I don't know. I never have to walk the whole way. Somebody always picks me up," Justine explained nonchalantly.

Andrea shot a sideways glance at Justine. A pick-up? Her mother had always told her never to get into a car with strangers. Never, ever. Not that she needed her mother to remind her. There were enough scary stories in the news to warn her of the dire consequences.

Less than a minute later a grey truck, driven by a middle-aged man, pulled up and stopped beside them. Justine greeted the man by name and climbed in, followed by a reluctant Andrea. After a few words with the driver about someone they both knew Justine, said,

"Joe, this is Andrea who's starting work today."

"Hello there," Joe greeted her warmly. Andrea responded with an uncertain "Hi," wondering who Joe was. Their journey didn't last long. The road ended in a huge car park. There were only a few cars in it at this time of the morning. They got out and walked towards a modern building with huge glass doors and a sign that said VISITOR RECEPTION CENTRE.

"Not that way," directed Justine, as Andrea headed for the door. "We're not supposed to go in there. That's for the public. We're staff."

Andrea followed her around to the side of the building, where a bus stood waiting with both doors open. Along with Joe and several other men and women, the girls filed in and soon the bus was heading down a narrow road.

"Doesn't anyone come to work in their own cars?" asked Andrea, thinking of Jackie's nifty little car from the night before.

"They don't allow cars anywhere near the fortress," explained Justine. "It would spoil the look of things. See? There it is over there."

Last night's rain had dwindled to a mist, out of which, on the far side of the bay, rose a fortress town from another age. Andrea could not take her eyes off the hazy panorama of gleaming slate roofs, tall brick chimneys, soaring spires, and massive grey stone walls. It was hard to believe that what she was seeing was a replica of a town that had stood here on this bleak, windswept peninsula beside the Atlantic Ocean nearly three hundred years ago. It seemed like pure magic to Andrea.

As the bus rolled along Justine chatted with another girl who was sitting across the aisle, a giggling conversation about someone who had recently cut her long hair short then dyed it hot pink. Andrea wished they would shut up. Their outbursts of laughter were spoiling her special moment. She continued to gaze out the bus window, enchanted by the vision of another world.

The bus stopped at a circular drive, and everyone got out and began walking along a broad pathway towards a wooden drawbridge that spanned a narrow river. On the far side Andrea recognized the Dauphin Gate, consisting of two massive stone towers with a huge wooden door between them. She had read that the original Dauphin Gate had been built to keep out the dreaded English. Andrea's ancestors had been English people who migrated to Newfoundland about the same time that the French were building this great fort in the New World. It gave her a strange feeling to realize that her people would not have been welcome here, that they might have been imprisoned or even killed. Why, she wondered, had the French and the English always been fighting? And why did they still seem to have trouble getting along?

The girls walked past two young men dressed in baggy blue-and-grey uniforms. Their role was that of eighteenth-century French soldiers, but they were still part of the twentieth century. One was sipping coffee from a styrofoam cup and the other was drinking Diet Pepsi out of a can. Their flintlock muskets were propped against the wall along with their tricorn hats.

"Hi, Dave! Hi, Jimmy!" called Justine.

"Have a nice day!" one of them replied.

"Break a leg!" added the other.

The girls continued along a gravel path beside the high, impenetrable wall that had once defended the people of this garrison against their enemies. How futile it seemed nowadays in a world full of aircraft and bombs and missiles. Yet how imposing it still looked. Andrea realized that no matter how many pictures one saw of a place, it was always a surprise when you finally got there. You could feel it then, as well as see it. Of course, the book of fortress photographs she had seen in her school library had not included the sound of the waves lapping in Louisbourg Harbour, the smell of salt water, or the wild voices of the seagulls. It took Andrea a moment or two to realize that something was missing. Then she got it. There were no power lines or telephone poles cluttering the horizon and no cars or trucks to dominate the scene.

They entered a labyrinth of orderly streets and stone buildings within the walls. Andrea had begun to imagine that she was sliding back in time, picturing herself as a resident of this place, when Justine stopped in front of a tall wooden fence and pushed open a well-disguised secret door.

"C'mon. Follow me," she directed.

"What is this?"

"It's Lartigue House. It's where we get into our costumes."

"What did you call it again?"

"Lartigue. It's named after the family who built the original house. All the houses here are named after the colonists who lived in them in 1744. That was the last peaceful year. After that the English attacked and things were never the same again."

"Couldn't we look around a bit more first?" Andrea asked.

"We're not supposed to walk around unless we're wearing our costumes. Besides, you've got the whole summer to see all the stuff. You'll get bored with it soon enough. Just follow me."

They entered an enclosed yard and walked around to the back door of an ancient-looking house. But it only looked old from the outside. Inside they found themselves in a large room lined with lockers—exactly the same kind that lined the halls in the school Andrea attended in Ontario.

"Mine's number ten and Jackie said yours is number thirteen," stated Justine as she hastily pulled off her T-shirt and jeans and shoved them in her locker. She grabbed a long-sleeved white blouse from a hanger and wriggled it over her head. Then she stepped into an ankle-length, olive-green skirt that fastened with a drawstring at the waist. Finally she tied a cotton apron over the skirt. Andrea sat and watched as her roommate transformed herself into a maiden from another time.

Jackie Cormier arrived just then, carrying an almost identical costume. The only difference was that the coarse, woollen skirt was a faded shade of dark blue.

"These ought to fit you, Andrea. But I forgot to ask your shoe size, so I brought three pairs for you to try."

"Size seven and a half," said Andrea as she examined the unattractive shoes she would have to wear. They were flat, black slippers with a strap across the instep that fastened with a button, like babies' shoes. The toes were broad and square.

"How do you tell left from right?" she asked as she thrust her foot into one of them.

"You don't," laughed Jackie. "They were the same back then. Believe it or not, poor people sometimes bought their shoes one at a time. Shoes used to be an expensive luxury for ordinary folks."

"They still are," Andrea remarked, remembering how much her new winter boots had cost last year.

"These aren't as comfy as sneakers, but you'll get used to them," said Justine stoically as she buttoned hers. Then she helped Andrea into her costume. Andrea felt slightly ridiculous. There was something about long skirts that always made her feel like a little girl, as if it were

Hallowe'en or she were making a game of trying on her mother's clothes.

"Very nice," nodded Jackie approvingly. "You suit the role. Now don't forget your bonnet."

Andrea had been fingering the white cotton bonnet. She was not sure which way it was supposed to sit on her head, and anyway she was hoping she could get away without wearing it at all. She didn't like wearing hats of any kind and this one was downright silly. It looked more like a large handkerchief than a hat.

"I bet you don't know why we have to wear these bonnets, do you?" teased Justine as she stood in front of the mirror adjusting hers.

"No, why?"

"Because we've got lice!" squealed Justine.

"The bonnet," explained Jackie, "was supposed to keep the lice at home, if you see what I mean. Thank goodness we have ways to get rid of them nowadays. Apparently everybody had them back then."

Voices and footsteps signalled the arrival of more people. A small boy and girl scrambled noisily into the locker room, followed by their mother.

"Good morning, Brittany. Good morning, Scott," Jackie greeted the children.

"Sorry we're a bit late," the mother apologized.

"We coulda got here faster, but Scott wouldn't eat his cereal," grumbled Brittany, who had blonde pigtails and looked about eight years old.

"I did so eat my cereal," protested her younger brother loudly.

"No quarrelling," their mother ordered.

"Children, I want you to meet Andrea. She's going to be working with you," said Jackie.

"Say hello," urged their mother.

"H'lo," they mumbled, glancing briefly at Andrea.

Andrea shook their hands and tried to look serious about her new responsibilities. The job she shared with Justine was the supervision of these, and other, children. Every day twelve youngsters helped to recreate life as it had been lived in 1744 in the Fortress of Louisbourg. They ranged in age from five to twelve and were members of a corps of junior volunteers who lived in nearby communities. Although they only "performed" during the summer months when the fortress was open to the public, they met regularly throughout the winter with instructors who taught them the children's games, music, dances, and handicrafts of eighteenth-century France.

Andrea and Justine were there to help them get into their costumes, to supervise games and lunches and snack times, to make sure they wore their capes on rainy days, and to keep track of the musical instruments they played, as well as the handmade dolls and the partly finished embroidery. Things had to keep running on time, whether it was the daily performance of a folk dance or being dispatched home on the bus at the end of the day.

The little girls wore costumes almost the same as those worn by Andrea and Justine. The boys wore white shirts with baggy pants, rigid wooden shoes, and black tricorn hats. Even the littlest boys had to wear those preposterous hats. Andrea wondered if she was going to have trouble persuading them to keep their hats on.

"It's the little kids who really bring this place to life," Jackie declared, as several more of them arrived. "I know you're going to enjoy working with them, Andrea, but since this is your first day here I suggest you take a look around and become familiar with your new surroundings. Justine can show you about. I'll keep an eye on the youngsters for now."

Nothing could have pleased Andrea more. Jackie was turning out to be a pal—one of those people who sensed what you needed before you got up your nerve to ask. Andrea put on her idiotic bonnet and buttoned her baby-doll shoes. The two girls quickly left the building and hurried out through the secret door in the fence.

CHAPTER FIVE ✤

By the time they reached the centre of the town, the first busload of visitors had arrived. Andrea barely noticed them. She was absorbed by the atmosphere of this ancient town with its walled gardens, beckoning doorways, and quaint dormer windows. Except for the tourists in their modern summer clothes, she really did feel as if she had stepped back into another age. It took a while for her to realize that the tourists were staring at her as well as at the buildings. Of course. She and Justine were as otherworldly in appearance as the make-believe soldiers at the gate. At first she felt self-conscious. A young couple with a baby in a stroller paused to look her over. A pair of grey-haired women grinned at her and snapped a photograph. What was she supposed to do? Smile back or what?

"You sort of ignore them," said Justine with a shrug. After one week on the job, Justine was already indifferent to the curious stares. "Working here is something like being in a play. We're part of the cast, but we're still ourselves, if you get what I mean. If somebody asks us a question we answer them, but otherwise we just go on about our business."

Andrea followed Justine past a long, wooden building with neat, shuttered windows. "So, I hear you won a writing contest," Justine remarked.

"Hmm-mm," Andrea acknowledged as casually as she could, uncertain whether her achievement would make Justine admire her or hate her. "That's how I got this job. The winners were offered summer jobs with Parks Canada."

"What a brain," Justine said in a voice that was neither praising nor condemning.

"I chose to come here. It's where I most wanted to be. So, what about you? How did you get the job?" Andrea asked.

"I heard about it because one of my cousins worked here a few years ago. So I applied. I guess I got lucky, because they hired me."

"Are you in French immersion?" Andrea asked.

"No, I want to specialize in science."

"Do you speak French at all?"

"Sure I do. Back home just about everybody speaks French as well as English. My great-grandfather spoke only French, but I didn't know him because he died before I was born. Now, my grandfather, he switches back and forth between English and French. But my mom...Hey, look where we are! Perfect timing," proclaimed Justine, abruptly changing the subject.

Andrea followed her down a lane leading into a yard, then in through the back door of a building. It was dim and warm inside and smelled delicious. This was the town bakery, known as the King's Bakery because the King of France had owned it, along with almost everything else in Louisbourg. As her eyes adjusted to the gloom, Andrea could see two men dressed in loose, white shirts and baggy pants, hauling loaves of fresh bread from an enormous stone oven. One of them was Joe, the man who had given them a ride earlier that morning. Joe was stacking dozens of loaves onto racks where they would cool. The other man poked a long-handled shovel into the interior of the great wall oven to retrieve more round loaves. They were twice as big as the loaves people buy in supermarkets now.

"Mmmm. Do I ever love the smell of fresh bread." Andrea sighed.

"Joe! Joe!" called Justine. "Can we have some, please?"

Joe looked up and recognized them. His face, hair, and clothes were dusted with flour. He ambled across the room with two chunks of warm bread and gave them to the girls. "There you go, eating up all the profits again," he chuckled.

"What did he mean?" asked Andrea as they headed down the street again, munching as they went.

"They sell this bread to the visitors," explained Justine.

"Maybe we shouldn't be eating it."

"Are you crazy? They've got tons of the stuff. They bake it every day. Anyway, I know Joe. I go to the same high school as his daughter. They're from L'Ardoise, not far from where I live."

"Where else can we go?" asked Andrea, wanting to see as much as possible.

"Well…let's see…" pondered Justine. "We could go and look at the parade square. There might be some soldiers hanging around. Or maybe the stables…that's kind of fun. Or the storehouse. Wait till you see the storehouse. You know, back when people really lived here, they brought over absolutely every single thing they needed from France so they could live as if they were in a town back home. You'd think they were heading into outer space; as if there was nothing here that anyone could use."

"So just what is that?" asked Andrea, pointing to an object in a doorway that had obviously not been imported from France in some other century.

"That? That's a movie camera. Did you never see one before? It's for making films," replied Justine, giving Andrea a sarcastic smile.

"I know that," Andrea laughed impatiently. "I mean, what's it doing here?"

"A bunch of people from away—from the States or England or some place—are making a movie. It's a story about the olden days. They got permission to film it here because, with all these authentic buildings and everything, it makes it look real," Justine explained.

A nice-looking young guy, wearing black sunglasses,

a plaid shirt, and faded jeans, emerged from the doorway, hoisted the camera and tripod onto his shoulder, and marched off down the street.

"Let's follow him," suggested Justine mischievously.

Keeping a discreet distance, the girls scurried along the street and turned a corner just in time to see the cameraman disappear through an archway and enter a doorway. A few seconds later they quietly opened the door and went inside. They could hear footsteps ascending a flight of stairs followed by the sound of a door being closed. They waited for a few minutes and climbed the stairs. At the top the closed door bore a sign that said NOT OPEN TO THE PUBLIC.

"Heck, we're not the public. We're staff," reasoned Justine as she cautiously pushed the heavy door open.

Andrea was not comfortable with Justine's boldness. She knew they weren't supposed to be there. She didn't want to get into trouble the very first day of her new job.

They found themselves in a large and elegant room that was a complete contrast to the pioneer atmosphere of the bakery. Here they were surrounded by antique French furniture embellished with silk upholstery and gilt. There was a large, multi-coloured oriental rug on the floor. Damask draperies the colour of rubies framed the elegant, tiny-paned windows.

"Hey, I like this," whispered Andrea.

"It's the governor's suite," said Justine in a hushed voice.

They could hear voices coming from the next room. They tiptoed to a doorway and peered in. The adjoining room was even larger and every bit as luxurious. At the far end, under a blaze of lights, stood a cluster of cameras and sound equipment, along with a group of people whose attention was focused on two actors, a man and a woman, who were looking intently into each other's eyes.

The man was dressed in a dark velvet jacket and a pale shirt with lace frills at the neck and wrists. His skin-tight white pants looked as if they would split if he sat down.

Perched on a dainty little chair, the woman was wearing a dress Andrea would have died for. It was made of some silky material the colour of roses and the long, puffed skirt cascaded over the floor. Her lace-trimmed bodice was cut so low in front that you could see… well, just about everything. Her hair, Andrea concluded, couldn't possibly have been real. It was as pale as a mushroom and piled up high in the shape of a haystack.

Andrea and Justine huddled together behind the folds of the draperies and kept as still as a pair of porcelain mice. They knew they weren't supposed to be there, but this was altogether too exciting to miss. A bearded man kept interrupting the male actor and making him say his lines over and over. At long last he apparently got it right because the gorgeous lady stood up, picked up her accordion-pleated fan, flicked it flirtatiously below her eyes, then glided gracefully away from her suitor and all the cameras and lights.

"That's a take!" called the bearded man who seemed to be in charge of things.

Andrea and Justine exchanged glances. Justine jerked her head in the direction of the door. This was obviously the right time to leave, while there was some commotion among the crew and the actors. They were nearly at the door when they heard a man's voice call out, "Hold on there!" They turned around to see the bearded man almost running towards them.

"Uh oh." Andrea gulped.

"I'm outta here," blurted Justine.

"Young ladies!" The man greeted them. "I want to talk to you."

"Sorry," Andrea apologized. "We just wanted to watch."

"And you enjoyed watching us at work, did you?" he asked.

The girls nodded.

"Well, I was watching you…out of the corner of my eye. You looked rather…appropriate…just the way a couple of servants might look if they happened to be eavesdropping on a conversation."

Both girls looked embarrassed. They really had been eavesdropping. And they had been caught.

"It just so happens we're looking for someone about your age and appearance to play a small role in this film.

I don't know if this is your cup of tea but, in case you'd care to give it a whirl…well, here's my card. I'm the director of this film," he explained in a rapid-fire British accent.

Andrea and Justine read the card, CHRISTOPHER GRUNDY, DIRECTOR, then looked at one another in amazement. They had expected a bawling out, at the very least.

"Well…thank you. That sounds…um…interesting," said Andrea, who was too surprised to know what else to say.

"We'd have to ask our supervisor," added Justine cautiously. "You see, our real job is to keep an eye on the little kids and help with the games and things, and wander around and look as if we lived here in the old days."

"Precisely what I have in mind," he agreed. He was a thin man with a thin face, and he wore a thick sweater of ivory-coloured wool. He pointed towards the busy crew. "That's my assistant over there. Let us know fairly soon if you'd like to be involved."

Andrea glanced across the room to see a muscular young man in a black T-shirt coiling a length of black cable. He had a long pony-tail the colour of the fur on an Irish setter. He appeared to be sharing some sort of joke with the glamorous star in the divine dress. She didn't look quite so elegant now. She had taken off her outrageous wig and her own hair was a tangled mess.

Meanwhile, the director was writing something down in his notebook. He ripped out the page and handed it to Andrea. "This is my assistant's name and phone number."

The paper read, "Penny Goodman."

"Penny?" questioned Andrea. "That guy's name is Penny?"

"I beg your pardon?" exclaimed Christopher Grundy. "I hasten to assure you that Penny is decidedly a female. There she is. Over there, beside the armoire."

Andrea had been looking at the wrong person. Penny was a shapely woman in beige slacks, a navy turtleneck, and horn-rimmed glasses. She was busy writing something in a notebook on her clipboard.

"Oops," laughed Andrea. "I thought you meant him, that guy over there, the one with the long hair."

"No, no. That's Calvin. He's the gaffer. Do tell us your decision as soon as possible, won't you?" he said commandingly and then turned and walked away to rejoin his crew. Andrea watched him go, then her gaze drifted back to Calvin and his copper-coloured hair. It couldn't be his real colour, could it?

As they descended the stairs, Andrea asked Justine, "What's a gaffer?"

"Haven't a clue."

The two of them hurried out of the building and rushed back towards Lartigue House. They didn't stop smiling. They could hardly believe their good luck.

CHAPTER SIX ⚜

Justine said she would ask permission for them to be in the film, but when it came right down to doing it she lost her nerve. "You ask, okay?" she pleaded, tossing the responsibility to Andrea. "I'll bet you're good at that kind of thing."

"Not especially," Andrea protested, but she mustered her courage and went to the administration office. It was located in Dugas House, a building that, from the outside, looked like a typical eighteenth-century French colonial home. Inside, it was a different story. Instead of the sparse, wooden furniture and open fireplaces that had sustained French families so long ago, this building was furnished with steel desks, swivel chairs, a row of gleaming filing cabinets, a computer, a fax machine, and several telephones. This was where decisions were made about the day-to-day concerns of running the Fortress of Louisbourg and where Jackie Cormier's office was.

Jackie listened carefully while Andrea described how she and Justine had been asked to play a role in the film. "Would it be all right if we accepted?" she asked tentatively.

There was a thoughtful pause while Jackie tapped her pen on her desk. "I don't see why not," she replied. "Film is another way of promoting the fortress, after all. As long as this won't take too much time away from your regular work…"

"They didn't say how long it would take."

"Tell me about it," said Jackie, nodding wearily. "Filmmakers seldom do know how long anything's going to take. I've worked with them before."

"All we have to do is stand behind some drapes and secretly listen to the governor's conversation with his fiancée. That shouldn't take very long," Andrea reasoned.

"That depends," said Jackie, raising a sceptical eyebrow, "on the length of the conversation. I hope it'll be fascinating."

"Well, it's not," replied Andrea. "We've already heard it. The governor had to repeat it over and over and over. It got boring."

"So you really were eavesdropping, were you?"

"Ohmigosh, no. It's just that we had to keep quiet while they were rehearsing. We couldn't help overhearing them," Andrea explained in a hurry.

"I'm sure it's not a state secret. It's part of the script. Okay, you and Justine go ahead. Sounds as if it could be fun."

Andrea left Jackie's office almost dancing with excitement. She and Justine really were going to act in a film, a major film, not a school play. She could hardly wait to tell Justine the good news.

A week later the two girls were called back to the governor's suite. The first person they saw was Calvin with the mahogany hair and the black clothes. He was up on a stepladder, tinkering with a tall light standard. Whatever it was that a gaffer did, it had something to do with wiring and lights.

"Um…hi," said Andrea. "We're going to be in the movie. We're supposed to see Penny Goodman about it."

"Well, ah declare," said Calvin, as he gave them both the once-over. "This's a day ah'll surely remember." He spoke in a slow, almost musical, accent of the sort you hear in old movies about cowboys and horses. Calvin's dark eyes darted from one girl to the other. His one gold earring was as flashy as his smile. "Ah'll go find Penny for you. Just who-all do ah say is he-ah?"

"Andrea and Justine."

"Andrea and Justine," he repeated carefully, as if their names were of great significance. "Don't y'all go 'way now."

He was back in two minutes, accompanied by a harassed-looking Penny Goodman carrying her clipboard. She glanced at the girls, but her mind was obviously on something else. "Be with you in a minute," she announced, and strode towards one of the cameramen, launching into an energetic discussion with him. When she came back, she seemed distracted. "Your costumes are okay, but you need make-up. Downstairs, to the left. And tell Charlene to make it snappy. We're behind schedule."

The make-up artist worked in a cramped room with one small window, a room normally used for storing fortress furniture. Tables and chairs had been shoved against a wall to make space for a couple of bright lights, a big mirror, a wheeled cart full of make-up, and a bulky reclining chair. In it was the actor who played the governor, still in white tights and velvet jacket. A cotton cape was draped around his shoulders. Charlene, a plump woman in a pink smock, was leaning over his face and brushing powder over his closed eyelids. Andrea had never seen a man's face covered in make-up before.

Charlene had chocolate-coloured skin and a halo of thick black hair. She glanced at Andrea and Justine and said, "Oh, Lordy, don't tell me there's two of you. I thought there was only one more."

The governor opened his powdered eyelids and looked over at them. "Good morning, ladies," he greeted them, oozing the artificial charm trained actors seem able to project even first thing in the morning.

"Lean back," ordered Charlene and brushed mascara on his eyelashes. Then she flicked off the make-up cape and announced, "You're done. Who's next?"

"You go first," said Andrea, nudging Justine.

"No, you," protested Justine.

"I want to watch how she does it," Andrea insisted.

Justine wiggled herself into the big chair. Charlene wrapped the make-up cape around her shoulders, then she stood back and took a long, analytical look at Justine's face before getting to work applying creams and powders in a subdued rainbow of pastel shades. Justine began to look older and considerably more glamorous. Charlene put the final touches to her work of art with a swoosh of mascara and a dab of bright lipstick. She stepped back to inspect her creation and nodded approvingly.

"What about your hair?" she enquired.

"What about it?" asked Justine. She was admiring her brand-new image in the mirror. She ran her fingers through her hair and patted it into shape.

"Oh, now I remember," said Charlene. "You two are going to wear some kind of hats, right?"

"Our bonnets," replied Andrea, pulling hers out of her pocket. "It's because we've got lice!"

"Lice!" cried Charlene "You better not."

Andrea was next. After Charlene had worked her magic Andrea took a long look at herself in the mirror, wondering if she could pass for eighteen. Maybe nineteen. Would her friends be able to recognize her when the film was shown? She hoped her name would be listed in the cast. Justine finally dragged her away from her daydreams, worried that they were going to be late.

"Mah eyes are buggin' outta mah head," declared

Calvin approvingly as he viewed the girls from halfway up the stepladder. "Li'l dahlins," he sang out, as if it was a fragment of some song he knew.

Andrea tried not to smile in case it left lines in her make-up. No guy had ever called her "darling" before.

At the other end of the drawing room the governor, whose real-life name was Brock Rutherford, sat uncomfortably on the little curved chair that his true love usually occupied. He was wearing glasses and reading a copy of the *Halifax Chronicle-Herald*. His screen fiancée, whose real name was Deborah Cluett, was again dressed in the divine gown and the towering white wig. She was standing by an open window with her elbows on the sill—smoking a cigarette!

"Eww. Disgusting," muttered Andrea.

Justine nodded and then said, "That Calvin guy has a funny accent."

"He's from the States," Andrea explained.

"Way down yonder y'awl," mimicked Justine, trying to imitate him without much success.

"Do you think he's cute?" Andrea asked.

They stood watching him while he adjusted a light reflector. Justine considered the matter for a minute. "Sort of. Not exactly. I don't like his hair."

"Let's move it!" ordered Penny. She positioned the two girls in the doorway while she gave instructions about the way they were to look as they spied on the governor and his fiancée. She coached them on the expressions they should wear when they glanced at one another with their shared secret.

"You're frightened by what you've heard and seen," she emphasized. "Remember, you are servants. No status. No job security. If you get caught listening in on the boss, it's…" she demonstrated by pulling her index finger across her throat as if it was a knife. "So you're curious, but you're also very nervous. Got it?"

The girls nodded, already looking nervous.

Penny stepped off to one side. The governor and his lady returned to their proper places, without the cigarette, the eyeglasses, or the newspaper.

"My heart is yours, my own sweet love."

"I pledge you mine."

"Then shall we rendezvous this very night?"

"Oh yes, my dearest."

"Oh, yuck," thought Andrea to herself. Did people ever really say this kind of thing to one another? Even if it was the eighteenth century it still sounded absurd. She would have laughed out loud except that the cameras were now pointing in her direction. She acted surprised. She acted alarmed. She exchanged a knowing look with Justine before the two of them nervously inched their way back behind the drapery.

"Cut!" called the director. "That's the right idea. Now, next time it would be better if you, ah…Anita…" He pointed to Andrea. He had forgotten her name. "Could you stand just a little to the left of the door? And you…

ah…" He pointed at Justine and didn't even attempt her name. "Ah…you could look a bit less startled. Not quite so much expression."

They did the scene again. And again and again. In the end it took over an hour for them to create the precise mood the director wanted. By the time they were finished Andrea was weary and hot and Justine was in an irritable mood. Their heavy clothes were damp and their make-up felt sticky as they endured the heat from the lights. They were relieved when they were finally thanked and told they could leave.

"Y'all don't have to hurry away now," suggested Calvin, smiling at Andrea as he gathered up an electric cable.

"We want to get out of our costumes. We're awfully hot," Andrea complained.

"Then we can get some pop," added Justine.

"That's a mighty fine idea," Calvin agreed. "Ah was wonderin' where a fella goes aroun' he-ah for refreshment. Maybe ah could buy you a Pepsi. Maybe ah'll call you up sometime."

Andrea tried not to look surprised. Was this guy asking both of them to go out with him? Or just one? Which one?

"'Low me to introduce mahself. Calvin Jefferson Lee. Ah'm the gaffer. New to these parts. Come from Alabama."

"Oh," remarked Justine, who couldn't think of

anything to say. She had never met anyone from Alabama before. Nor had Andrea.

"Sure...we could go out...sometime," replied Andrea uncertainly.

"And you are Miss Andrea...?"

Andrea suppressed a giggle. "Miss," for heaven's sake. It was almost as old-fashioned as the governor's dialogue. "Baxter," she finally managed. "Andrea Baxter."

"I'm Justine Marchand," Justine announced. "We'd better go now. We room together at the Northeast Bed and Breakfast."

When they were aboard the bus heading back to town, Andrea asked her roommate, "Think I should go out with him?"

"Up to you."

"He is cute, isn't he?"

"I think he's kind of old for you."

"How old is he?"

"Ask him."

"I can't."

"I wouldn't worry about it. He might never call anyhow."

"I don't care," Andrea lied.

"Let's go for some pop," suggested Justine a few minutes later as they trudged up the main road of the real-life town of Louisbourg.

"Right now?"

"Sure. They're gonna die up at the store when they see us made up like this."

"Uh oh. The make-up. Maybe we should go home first and wash it off," suggested Andrea, suddenly aware of how unnatural they must look.

"Who cares?" shrugged Justine. "I just want to see the look on that guy's face when we walk in there like this."

"What guy?" asked Andrea.

"You know."

"No, I don't."

"He works there sometimes."

"Oh, that guy. Curly hair. Wears those round glasses. Never smiles. Right?"

"Cory is his name."

"You like him, don't you?"

"I never said that."

"You do so like him."

"I never said...all I said was I wanted to...oh, never mind. I just want a Coke, okay?"

"Let's go."

When they reached the store, it was to discover that Cory was not working that day. Vivian, the woman who owned the store, was behind the counter instead. She greeted them cheerfully and asked them where they were going that evening, seeing that their faces were so lavishly made up. That only added to Justine's disappointment. They weren't going anywhere. By then Andrea merely felt self-conscious. Theatrical make-up simply didn't look right when you were wearing a sweatshirt that said BEAVER CANOE.

Disheartened that Cory was not around, Justine downed her Coke in a hurry. Andrea gulped a 7-Up and bought a chocolate bar, and they left. Justine was silent as they walked back. It wasn't until they were in the bathroom washing away the final traces of their brief acting career that her downcast mood began to improve.

"So, ah yew goin' to go ay-out with him...Calvin Jeff-ah-son Lee?" she asked, mocking his accent.

"Don't bug me. I dunno."

"I just thought of something. When he sees you without your make-up and your fortress costume, he might think you're...too young or something."

"I'm not too young," Andrea almost shouted.

"Just kidding."

"Besides, I can always make myself look older."

"How?"

"I'll get a grey wig, and a walking cane, Aunt Roberta's orthopaedic shoes, and my mom's reading glasses and..."

"And he'll think he's going out on a date with his grandmother," giggled Justine.

"Right."

"I dare you."

"Well, he has to ask first."

CHAPTER SEVEN ❦

There was a knock on the bedroom door. "Phone call
for Andrea," announced Roberta, who then clumped
heavily back down the stairs. Andrea opened her eyes
and looked at her alarm clock. It was 7:20 AM. Why
would he call her at this unromantic hour of the day?
She got up, yanked her bathrobe over her pyjamas,
dashed into the hall, and picked up the phone.

"Hi," she said, hoping she sounded as if she had been
awake for ages.

"Hi, sweetie," came the voice of her mother.

"Mom!" she exclaimed. "It's awfully early."

"It is. And it's even an hour earlier in Ontario, but I
just felt like calling you before the day got started. I miss
you, you know. Sometimes I worry about you. I know
that's silly but..."

"I'm fine, Mom. Honestly. I've been meaning to write
to you. It's just that I've been busy, very busy," Andrea
yawned. It was an effort to think of anything interesting to
say when she had been awake for only a couple of minutes.
For a while she simply listened as her mother chatted.

"How do you like your new job?"

"I like my job. I like my boss. I like my roommate. But the big news is that I got to play a part in a movie."

"A movie?"

"Yes, a film is being shot in the Fortress of Louisbourg because the story is set way back in history and the fortress looks absolutely right for that. Justine, my roommate, was in it too. We were supposed to be servants. It wasn't a very big role."

"How wonderful! When can I see it?"

"Not for quite a while. They're still working on it. And we're back to our real jobs," Andrea explained, a bit wistfully.

"What's the weather like down there?" her mother asked. She always asked that.

Andrea hadn't even looked outdoors yet. She went to the top of the stairs, where she could see the sky through a small window. It was beginning to rain. "It's raining, Mom," she replied dismally, not looking forward with any joy to the prospect of a damp day full of restless little kids and no likelihood of seeing Calvin.

"Too bad. The sun's shining here."

"Anyway, Mom, I'd better go. I have to get dressed and then eat and get to work. I promise I'll write and tell you more about it, okay?"

"Okay. Take care. Stay out of trouble."

"Mu-um. Stop worrying about me."

"Brad sends his love."

"Thanks for calling."

"Bye."

Andrea and Justine were gulping a fast breakfast when Jackie Cormier dropped by to offer them a lift to work. By then a steady rain was pelting down. When they reached the fortress parking area, the girls climbed out of the car, but Jackie remained inside, along with her five-year-old son, Kenzie.

"Aren't you coming with us?" asked Andrea.

"I'll be along later. I'm going to Sydney first to see my mother. She's in a nursing home there."

"Oh. Too bad."

"It is. She's got Alzheimer's disease. She has good days and bad days. It's hard for us sometimes, especially for Kenzie. He never knows whether his grandma will recognize him or not."

Andrea thought about how sad that must be. Her own mother was still young and healthy enough to worry about her.

"Anyway," Jackie continued, "I'll be back soon. And I'm looking forward to a relatively quiet day without that film crew in my hair. They always seem to need something—permission for this or that, or else they want to borrow things, or rearrange the furniture. Today they're spending the entire day filming in the chapel."

"Is that so? Thanks for the ride, Jackie," Andrea called as she swung the car door shut. She ran to catch up with Justine, who was already on board the bus.

The volunteer children soon began to arrive in plastic raincoats and wet sneakers. They donned their costumes and prepared for a day that promised indoor activities only. There would be many games of checkers. Some of the girls would work on their embroidery. There might even be a session of blowing bubbles through the stalks of angelica plants, a simple pastime that the colonial children had invented using the tough, celery-like stalks of a flowering plant that grew in their gardens.

However, Andrea had a plan of her own. Once the children were dressed in their costumes, she sprang it on them.

"Kids! I've got an idea for this morning. Instead of just hanging around and doing handicrafts, I thought it would be fun if we walked up to the chapel for a while."

Justine stared at her in utter surprise. "In the rain? Are you crazy? Why on earth do you want to do that?"

"Because…the chapel is so beautiful. It's peaceful and it's…I can't explain…I was just in the mood for…"

"For praying?"

"Wouldn't you like to go? You're a Catholic, aren't you?"

"Yes, but we don't usually go to church on Tuesdays."

"Well, it wouldn't hurt. I bet the kids would like it for a change. Okay, who wants to come with me to the chapel?" Andrea asked enthusiastically.

A chorus of agreement greeted the idea of going somewhere. Justine made no further comment. Possibly

Andrea had a serious problem, she thought, or a terrible secret she couldn't discuss with anyone. Maybe she needed to sit in the chapel and meditate, although why she would want to do so with a dozen young children tagging along was something of a mystery. They wrapped the children in their capes and hats and soon they were all trudging through the drizzle towards the chapel.

When they reached the chapel, everyone except Andrea was surprised to see that the little church was anything but a haven of tranquility. Andrea managed to look appropriately amazed at the blaze of lights, the camera equipment, and the glamorous Deborah Cluett standing outside the door, dressed to kill, and—wouldn't you know it—smoking a cigarette.

"Hi there!" she greeted them, as if they were old friends. "This is my wedding day. Would you like to watch me get married?" she invited, as she butted her cigarette on the wet ground underneath a dainty white shoe. Her wedding dress was even more spectacular than the dress she had worn the previous day. It was the ivory colour of old lace, with an embroidered bodice and a long, full skirt that billowed out over a hooped petticoat. A delicate veil hung from the top of her wig to her smooth shoulders. Andrea would have given a lot to try on that costume. She wondered where it was kept when Deborah wasn't wearing it.

"Sure is a beautiful dress," Andrea managed to say.

"Yes, but I wish it was more comfortable. It has a

whalebone corset inside the waist, and I can hardly breathe it's so tight," Deborah complained.

The bride returned to the chapel, while an entourage of children and Andrea and Justine stood and watched from the doorway. Deborah took her place in front of the altar, while her attentive audience stood silently against the back wall.

"Andrea," whispered Justine sympathetically, "it's not very peaceful here right now. We can come back some other time."

"It's fine. Really," Andrea reassured her, then turned to the children. "Now not a peep out of anyone, understand? This is a wedding, and if we're very quiet we can watch them film it."

In front of the altar stood a gaunt-looking actor dressed as a priest. He was being fussed over by Charlene, the make-up artist, who kept dabbing more powder on his bald head. Nearby Mr. Grundy, the director, was engaged in some sort of argument with a frowning Penny Goodman. Deborah, the bride, was sitting on a folding chair blotting her hairline with a paper towel and complaining about her itchy wig. The governor, who was about to marry her, was immaculately dressed in a royal blue brocade coat and those same clingy white tights. However, he looked as if he couldn't have cared less about the wedding. He was sitting on the top step of the pulpit, leafing through a sports magazine. Near him stood Calvin Jefferson Lee. He was looking in the opposite direction, as if something were about to happen in the farthest corner of the chapel.

Justine nudged Andrea and whispered, "They certainly didn't waste any time getting married, did they? They only fell in love on Friday and here they are getting married on Tuesday."

"Honestly!" giggled Andrea. "They don't film scenes in the sequence that the audience sees them. In the story, there could have been a long time, maybe a whole year, between when they first met and when they finally got married. They're probably filming this wedding today because it's raining and they can't work outside."

"I know that!" said Justine. "I was making a joke."

Christopher Grundy heard the buzz of conversation and squinted past the bright lights to see who it was. Andrea was silent immediately and her face turned pink with embarrassment. Only a minute earlier she had been admonishing the children to keep quiet and now she and Justine were the ones to be caught making a noise.

"Oh, it's you." He gave a slight wave. "Don't go away. I want to talk to you."

Andrea and Justine exchanged an apprehensive look. Mr. Grundy continued talking to Penny until they had apparently resolved their problem. Then he spent another couple of minutes explaining something to the priest.

"I'm going to re-name Mr. Grundy 'Mr. Grumpy,'" Andrea announced quietly. "That guy never smiles."

"Grumpy Grundy," echoed Justine with a smirk.

Just then he turned and strode to the doorway where Andrea and Justine were surrounded by a huddle of children in damp capes. "The very girls I wanted to see," he greeted them. "It appears we have another role for you in this film sometime soon. Are you interested?"

Too surprised to speak, Andrea and Justine nodded their heads.

"Splendid. Let's see now…you are Anna and you… ah…are Christine," he ventured.

"Andrea," corrected Andrea.

"Justine," corrected Justine.

"You'll be hearing from us. Penny's got your names written down somewhere," he said, and promptly returned to the altar to have a few words with the restless bride.

"Gawd," Deborah groaned loudly. "This damn dress is so uncomfortable. I can't wait to get it off."

"Not till after the weddin', Deborah dahlin'," joked Calvin Jefferson Lee.

"From the top!" shouted the director imperiously. Calvin and the rest of the crew stepped off to one side. The bride and groom took their places beside each other. The priest opened his prayer book and read something in Latin. The filming began.

By the time the third take was completed, the youngest children were starting to shuffle their feet and whisper among themselves. Reluctantly, Andrea herded them all outdoors. It was better to leave now, before they were asked to leave. She was annoyed that Calvin hadn't even noticed she had been there. However, she had seen him. What's more, she was now going to play an additional role in the film. He wouldn't have any choice but to notice her next time.

"Isn't it wild?" giggled Justine as they all hurried along the road in the dwindling rain. "Maybe they really are in love."

"Of course they're not," Andrea insisted.

"Could be," Justine persisted.

"I happen to know that Brock Rutherford is already married to someone else. They're just acting."

"Actors get divorced any time they feel like it, and then they get married to somebody else. Everyone knows that," Justine declared.

"Not all of them. And I'll tell you something, if I ever get married—and I'm not sure I'm going to—it will be for keeps," Andrea said emphatically.

"Same here," echoed Justine. "But if I were Deborah Cluett, I wouldn't want to marry that guy anyway. He's much too old for her."

"You want to marry Cory up at the store."

"Oh shut up."

CHAPTER EIGHT ✦

The following day was as bright as the previous one had been dreary. A brisk west wind banished the clouds and rain. A galaxy of waving wildflowers could be seen in the fields surrounding the walled town.

On days like this the sea was the colour of sapphires, a fathomless, deep blue, broken only by the bursting white spray where distant waves collided with offshore rocky islands. Even if there had been no Fortress of Louisbourg, Andrea imagined that it would have been a fulfilling experience for tourists just to stare at the ever-changing Atlantic Ocean. She never got tired of looking at it herself.

Andrea turned back towards the town, where a busload of visitors could be seen crossing the drawbridge by the Dauphin Gate. Suddenly she noticed Justine in front of Lartigue House. She was talking to a nice-looking guy, chatting to him in a way that suggested she knew him, that he was more than a visitor asking for directions. Did she have a crush on someone else? What about Cory? Andrea ambled slowly towards them, curious to get a better look at whoever he was. Eventually Justine saw her and waved enthusiastically.

"Andrea, come on over!"

Andrea approached nonchalantly, not wanting to appear too eager.

"Surprise, surprise. This is my brother Marc. Marc, this is Andrea."

"H'lo there," said Marc shyly, with a quick half-smile.

"Hi," Andrea greeted him. Marc was a large, imposing-looking fellow, dressed in a new pair of jeans and an oversized, white T-shirt. He had short, dark hair, the same colour as Justine's. He had dimples when he smiled.

"So guess what?" asked Justine, without stopping long enough for Andrea to guess anything. "Marc drove up to Sydney airport to pick up a couple of exchange students from Quebec and it turned out they missed their connecting flight out of Halifax, so now they won't get here until this afternoon on another flight. Meanwhile, Marc had to hang around, so that's why he came over here."

"Helps to pass the time," explained Marc.

"Well, yeah, there's lots to see," Andrea agreed.

"You gonna stay for lunch?" Justine wanted to know.

"Nah, I better be on my way. I can get a sandwich at the airport," said Marc.

"Anyway, we should go too. Almost performance time. I'll see you in a few weeks," concluded Justine.

"See ya," said Marc, and then, as he walked away, he turned and added, "Nice to meet you."

"Same here." Andrea smiled.

Every morning at 11:30 when the weather was fine the children performed for fortress visitors. A trio of boys played tunes on a recorder, a drum, and a tambourine, while a circle of girls danced a traditional French step vaguely similar to the square dancing of today. Visitors loved it. They always gathered around to watch and to take lots of photographs.

One sunny morning it dawned on Andrea that this little performance hadn't been invented for tourists. This had been the reality in the days before people had television or videos or amplified music. In this distant outpost people had had to rely on themselves for entertainment. It occurred to her that little children would have enjoyed this uncomplicated dance and simple music the way they enjoyed taped music and movies today. Was it possible they could have enjoyed it more? In this fortress community the performers and the audience would have been acquainted with one another. If anyone had a special talent, then everyone else would have known about it. No one would have had to wait a lifetime to be discovered.

"You want to know something?" Andrea confided to Justine as they observed the children. "I once thought about becoming a video star—well, maybe not a star exactly, but doing some professional acting or singing."

"You did? So did I," admitted Justine.

"I was in a play at school," Andrea reminisced. "It was

called *Lady Windermere's Fan*. It was a lot of work, but I didn't mind because I enjoyed doing it. There were four performances, and after the last one there was a terrific party. I didn't get to bed until two o'clock in the morning."

"I was in a play at school too. It was a drama to teach kids to take care of their teeth. I played the part of the toothbrush," Justine said proudly.

Andrea made no comment. That didn't sound like a very interesting part, pretending to be a toothbrush.

"The trouble is my mom doesn't think that acting is a good career choice. She says there aren't that many jobs around. So I thought about it for a while and decided I'd be an airline flight attendant. I love to travel."

"I changed my plans too," Justine agreed. "What I really like best in the world is animals. So I've decided to become a veterinarian."

"I love animals too. I wish I had a dog. I might be getting one in the fall."

"We've got a dog. And three cats. And seven cows. And twenty-two hens. And a pig," counted Justine.

"You're lucky. I wish we had room for lots and lots of animals."

"Do you want to come home with me sometime? You could see our dog and meet everyone. In August there's going to be a big party on my birthday. And my twin sister's birthday too, of course."

"Sure. I'd like that," said Andrea enthusiastically.

"We can catch the bus from Sydney. It only takes about an hour from there."

The children completed their little show and the tourists clapped enthusiastically before dispersing to see other things. Andrea glanced along the quay and her heart suddenly skipped a beat. Calvin Jefferson Lee was striding towards them, his long hair blowing in the wind.

"Found you at last," he said breathlessly to Andrea, as if he had been looking for her all his life.

"We haven't exactly been hiding," Justine remarked quickly.

"Ah been lookin' for Andrea Baxter all over this burg, and he-ah she is, ta-dum!"

A shiver ran down Andrea's spine. "What's up?" she asked as calmly as if Calvin searching for her was an everyday occurrence.

"Penny Goodman wants to see you. Over on the parade square."

"Now?"

"Right now."

"Just me?"

"Just you."

So Calvin was only the messenger.

"It's almost lunchtime," Andrea protested. "We have to supervise."

"You'd better go. I'll watch the kids till you get back," Justine volunteered, but without a smile.

Andrea had to walk faster than usual to keep up with

Calvin, who charged through the crowds with a long, loping stride. He was a lot taller than she was.

For a time he didn't say a word. Finally he remarked, "I s'pose you got a boyfriend back home?"

Andrea wasn't sure how to reply. Would he be impressed if she said she did have one? Would he think there was something wrong with her if she didn't? She decided the truth was the best choice.

"Not at the moment."

"A purty gal like you and you haven't got a guy!" said Calvin in mock horror. "Why, ah might have a chance after all."

"Who knows?" said Andrea as casually as she could, tossing her head in a way she hoped would tell him she wasn't tripping over her shoelaces to go out with him.

When they reached the main intersection of the town, Calvin turned the corner to the left.

"Ah'm off to see a man about a hoss," he chuckled.

What did he mean? Was that some kind of code meaning he had to go to the bathroom, or was he...

"We gotta hire a pony from the stable for tomorrow's shootin'. S'long, dahlin'." Andrea continued up the road by herself. When she reached the parade square, she couldn't see Penny Goodman anywhere. The place was deserted except for Grumpy Grundy way down at the far end. He waved and beckoned her to join him.

"Hello there, Angela. Just the girl I wanted to see!"

"It's Andrea."

"Of course it is. I need a word with you without your friend…what's-her-name."

"Justine."

"Right. I'll be brief. It now appears that we have a more expanded role coming up. The lady's maid is going to be somewhat more significant to the plot. We've revised the script, and we have a scene where the maidservant will be transporting an important secret message. It calls for dramatic looks—bewilderment, fear, relief—the sort of thing that you do rather well, if I may say so. Do you think you could handle this role?"

Andrea swallowed and thought about it for two seconds. "I think so."

"Sorry we don't have another role for your friend. Josephine's quite good, but—"

"Justine."

"You have what we're looking for."

His cellular phone rang, and he reached into his briefcase to retrieve it. It was a call from Penny Goodman, who was supervising a scene in the garden behind the engineer's house. "Yes, Penny. Yes, she's right here and we've discussed the part. I believe she intends to do it." He looked Andrea in the eye and nodded his head, asking for confirmation. Andrea nodded back.

"A done deal then," he told Penny, and continued to talk to her about production details. After a while he perched the phone on his shoulder and said, "Thank you for coming by, Amanda. We'll be in touch."

"I'm Andrea."

"So you are."

When the day's work was over, Andrea and Justine caught the bus back to town. As usual they walked to Vivian's store for some pop. It gave them something to do before supper and, of course, Justine had a chance to see Cory—if he happened to be on duty that day. She never knew for sure.

"I phoned home," said Justine, "and my brother Marc said he'd come up and get us in the car when we get our days off in August. That way we won't have to wait around for the bus."

"Sounds great," Andrea agreed.

"And I was thinking. I might even invite one or two kids from around here. It's my birthday, after all."

"Cory. Cory. Cory," teased Andrea.

Justine blushed. "Shut up," she muttered, and changed the subject. "So what did Penny want? Do we have to do that stupid scene over again?"

"No, we don't. Actually, Penny wasn't there. Just Grumpy."

"Oh, him. What did he have to say?"

"Nothing really…except there's another scene to do."

"Ohhh. Gimme a break," groaned Justine. "All those hot lights. All that waiting around. All that make-up.

I can't STAND it," she proclaimed in mock dismay, holding the back of her hand to her forehead and looking up towards the sky.

"Actually…as it happens…this time there's only one part…for one servant…for me," Andrea explained haltingly.

"Oh," said Justine frostily, and didn't utter another word until they arrived at Vivian's store. Luckily Cory was behind the counter and that thawed Justine's icy mood. The girls were the only customers, so there was time to chat. And, as it turned out, there was a lot to talk about. The big news was that there had been a robbery at a convenience store in the town of Dominion, not far away. Cory had just heard all about it from the guy who drove the bread-delivery truck.

"The police figure the man was mainly after cigarettes," he explained earnestly. "He took nineteen cartons of them and also stole twenty-five videos, along with all the money in the cash drawer."

"How did he get in?" Andrea wanted to know.

"They think that maybe he hid, that he was inside the building at closing time. The fellow on duty that night had to step outside because there's a gas pump out in front. A couple of cars came by for gas just before he closed the store. Somebody could have walked in and hidden in a cupboard maybe."

"Scary," commented Justine, sipping her Coke very, very slowly.

Another customer came in, and Cory got busy slicing baloney, cutting a chunk of cheese, and signing out a video.

"We'd better go," Andrea suggested.

"How's everything up at the fortress?" enquired Cory as they headed for the door.

"Come and see for yourself," Justine suggested coyly.

"I might," agreed Cory with a hint of a smile.

As they walked back, Justine became quiet again. The two girls ate their supper in silence and after that Justine slumped in a chair in front of the television, watching a re-run of *North of 60*. Andrea went upstairs and washed her hair. Justine was obviously hurt that she hadn't been asked to play another role in the film and Andrea had. It wasn't my fault, Andrea reasoned. I wasn't the person who made that decision. Why does she have to take it out on me with her big sulk?

When they were getting ready for bed, Justine announced importantly, "As soon as I finish grade twelve I'm going to apply."

"Apply what?"

"Apply to the University of Prince Edward Island, to the veterinary college there."

"Terrific," Andrea said enthusiastically, and listened patiently as Justine mentioned the high marks she always got in science and talked about her interest in farm animals. At least Justine was speaking to her.

They got into their beds and Andrea leaned over to

turn out the light. "Hey, Juss, when did you say your brother was coming to get us?"

"He'll let us know," she yawned, and then turned her back on Andrea and snuggled her head into her pillow.

"G'night, Juss."

Justine didn't say anything.

Andrea lay awake for a long time.

CHAPTER NINE ❖

"Get set! Now ruuuuun!" bellowed Grumpy Grundy.

Andrea hoisted her long skirt just above her ankles, not too far above them, but exactly the way Penny had demonstrated. Then she darted fairly gracefully down the gradual slope of the parade square. As she reached Maison de la Plagne she paused and glanced back with a well-rehearsed anxious expression on her face. Then she disappeared around the corner.

By the time the morning's work was over, Andrea had run down that same slope and around that same corner a total of nine times. How could such an uncomplicated scene possibly have so many variations, particularly as she wasn't required to speak one single word? She ran and ran and ran. Grumpy was turning out to be an insufferable perfectionist. He rarely appeared to be pleased with anything that Andrea or the other actors did. If it hadn't been time to break for lunch, Andrea felt sure she would have been asked to run down that boring parade square a tenth time, an eleventh time, a twelfth time…

Everyone in the film crew was entitled to a one-hour break for lunch. They carted their equipment to a nearby building then drifted away. Andrea watched them, hoping for a glimpse of Calvin, but he wasn't among them. It must have been his day off. Just her luck. She returned to the staff lunchroom, where Justine and twelve little children were sitting around the table eating their sandwiches. Justine greeted Andrea with an impassive "Hi" and not another word. She didn't enquire about the morning film shoot. She didn't ask about Calvin. She didn't ask about anything. She focused her attention on the children and made sure they cleaned up the mess after they had eaten.

After a while Andrea felt courageous enough to ask, "Hey, Juss, are you going up to the store for some pop after work?"

"I'll see," replied Justine stiffly.

Andrea could feel a knot tightening in her stomach. It became an effort to swallow her peanut butter sandwich. In the end she couldn't finish it. She was in no mood to work on the film that afternoon, but she knew she had to. It was a good thing the script didn't call for smiles or laughter. She could never have managed that, not today. In her next scene, during which she was still fleeing across town with her secret message, she had to portray fear, to look as if she thought she was being pursued by someone dangerous. She had spent a lot of time in front of the bathroom mirror every night for two weeks past, practising expressions of fear, anxiety, and exhaustion. She had wisely locked the bathroom door in case Justine barged in and observed what she was doing.

By the middle of the afternoon it wasn't a challenge to look exhausted. Eventually she was rescued by the weather. This particular scene had to be filmed in fog. There had been lots of that in the morning, but by three o'clock the wind had shifted and, to the delight of everyone except Christopher Grundy, the sun began to shine. Completion of the scene was postponed until the next foggy day.

Andrea returned to her regular job for the rest of the afternoon. Jackie was generous in letting her take part in the film, but Andrea never imagined that it would occupy so much time. Justine had taken most of the children for a walk among the ruins beyond the fortress, so Andrea didn't have much to do. She used the time to tidy the costume cupboard and then she caught an early bus to town. She was relieved to get back ahead of Justine so she could wash off every trace of the theatrical make-up before her roommate came home. When Justine did return she was still aloof, but Andrea was determined not to let it get to her. Together they walked to the store in gloomy silence while Andrea prayed silently that Cory would be on duty when they got there.

And he was. However, there were five other customers in the store, so he was kept busy ringing up sales, stuffing things into plastic bags, checking out videos, and selling lottery tickets. One by one the customers left, all except one fellow who slouched against the pop cooler while he read a magazine from the rack.

Andrea finished her 7-Up and tossed the can into the garbage pail. Justine, who could sip a Coke more slowly than anyone else in the world, stopped reading the community notices on the bulletin board and meandered back towards the counter where Cory was finally alone, arranging a stack of videos on a shelf.

Andrea thoughtfully kept her distance. She knew what it meant to Justine to have a private chat with Cory, even though her moody friend always insisted she didn't give a hoot. She did so. Andrea walked over to the magazine rack, selected a copy of *Canadian Living*, and pretended to be reading an article describing how to dry wildflowers, a subject that didn't interest her at all. She was really listening to Justine talking to Cory, telling him something that one of the tourists had said to her that day.

"...no kidding. That's what he asked. He wanted to know why didn't they build this fortress over near the Bras d'Or lakes instead of here, because there isn't as much fog over there. Also—get this—he said it would have been handier to the TransCanada Highway as well."

"Jeez," Cory guffawed. "So what did you say?"

"I told him there was no highway in 1717, the year that the king of France decided to build here. I mean, they hadn't even invented cars then. People travelled in ships. Louisbourg has an awesome harbour. I pointed to it, but the fog was so thick this morning we couldn't see it."

"Some people!" Cory snorted.

"Dumb de–dumb dumb," trilled Justine.

Andrea turned to put the magazine back on the rack. She'd learned everything she needed to know about dried flower arrangements. She headed back to the counter, paid Cory for her pop, then tactfully suggested to Justine that they would miss their supper if they didn't head back.

Justine swallowed the last drop of her Coke, paid for it, and left the store reluctantly. At least by then she was in a better mood, almost her normal self.

Next morning there was another early phone call for Andrea. She put on her bathrobe, padded out into the hall, and picked up the phone. It was Penny Goodman.

"Andrea? You do know how to swim, don't you?"

What kind of a question was that so early in the day?

"Sure, Penny," she replied. "I took lessons for ages. I got my intermediate badge, and I even started working on my senior's. Why?"

"More script revisions. We've got a scene coming up that requires filming you in some sort of boat. There's no danger, of course, but we just wanted to be sure you could swim if you had to. Are you comfortable about being in a boat in the harbour?"

"You bet. My uncle in Newfoundland has a fishing boat, and last summer I spent a lot of time in it. And before that there was another time…"

"Great," Penny cut her off. "Just what we wanted to hear. I'll get back to you. Bye."

When Andrea arrived at the locker room that morning, she found Kenzie Cormier and another little boy fighting on the locker room floor.

"Kenzie! Scott! You boys stop it this minute!" she shouted, yanking them apart.

"He took my shoes!" accused Scott fiercely.

"I never did!" Kenzie loudly insisted.

"Boys! Stop it! The shoes are all the same anyway. Maybe Kenzie put yours on by mistake," Andrea consoled.

"He did it on purpose," protested Scott.

"I doubt that very much," Andrea said firmly. "Kenzie, if those happen to be Scott's shoes, I want you to give them back and then you and I will find another pair for you, okay?"

Grudgingly Kenzie kicked off the wooden shoes and left them on the floor for Scott. He followed Andrea downstairs in his stocking feet. Having just turned five, Kenzie was the youngest member of the entire volunteer corps. He spent Wednesdays and Fridays at the fortress. The other weekdays he stayed with a babysitter in town. He was quite a handful, although Andrea wouldn't have admitted that to Jackie. She didn't want her boss to think she couldn't cope with any child in her charge, especially not Jackie's son.

Andrea hunted around in the costume cupboard and found another pair of wooden sabots that almost fitted Kenzie. She stuffed some straw into the toes of the rigid shoes, using the same method that fortress dwellers had once used to ensure a good fit. She got him into his costume in time to join the other children. Kenzie spent the next half hour running after a couple of the bigger boys who were playing hoop and stick. This was another game that had been played by children who grew up here long ago. The only people who played it nowadays were the volunteer corps at the fortress. All they needed was a simple wooden hoop, the kind that was once used by barrel makers, and a stick. The object was to keep the hoop rolling as long as possible by prodding it with the stick. A lot of running was required to prevent the hoop from falling over. It was the perfect game for overly energetic little boys.

Andrea watched as the children darted along the quayside, laughing and shouting as the hoops continued on their wobbly courses. At moments like this, she sometimes indulged in a daydream that she was actually living her life here that last, peaceful summer back in 1744. The longer she worked here the more she thought about that distant world when there had been no cars, no radios, no computers, no telephones, no washing machines, no hairdryers, no pop music, no magazines.

They didn't even have organized sports in those days, unless hoop and stick could be classified as a sport. There were very few books. Only the children of wealthy parents learned how to read. School was a luxury, the way ballet classes and riding lessons were today.

She liked to fantasize about living in a place where there were no schools. Imagine—never having to pay attention to a teacher or do your homework. But what would she have been doing instead? On a summer day like this, keeping an eye on children playing wasn't a bad way to pass the time. Yet it wouldn't all have been like this. She would have had to spend many hours scrubbing, knitting, and sewing—work that was now done by machines. There were some real disadvantages too, like head lice and scratchy clothes, and sleeping on a mattress stuffed with straw, not to mention the absence of certain things, like antibiotics and anesthetics if you became ill.

There was one other thing that Andrea couldn't quite picture for herself. Young women were sometimes married at her age. They might even be mothers by the time they were fifteen. A wife. A mother. Could she possibly...? Well, someday. Not yet.

Her fantasy came to an abrupt end with the pitiful sound of Kenzie bawling his eyes out. He was lying on the ground, clutching his knee and making a terrible fuss. Andrea rushed over, stood him up, and inspected his bleeding knee.

"I f-f-fell down!" he wailed.

"Come on," she said, putting her arm around him. "It'll be okay. We'll go and wash this off and get you a nice Band-Aid."

"'Kay," he sobbed and limped after her, tears streaming down his face.

There was a first-aid kit in the staff room for minor emergencies like this. Andrea dabbed his knee with a wet cloth, then covered the scrape with three Band-Aids. Kenzie finally stopped crying. He liked Band-Aids.

"Want my mommy," he demanded solemnly.

"She's over in her office. Let's go and show her your new Band-Aids."

Jackie gave her little boy a hug and told him how brave he was. She even found a toffee in her desk drawer, which cheered him up. As Andrea and Kenzie were about to leave, Jackie said, "I guess you heard what happened up the road last night?"

"No, what?"

"That little shop…in town here…"

"Vivian's?"

"Yes, that's the one. They were robbed."

"Robbed!" cried Andrea. "When?"

"I haven't got the whole story. It happened at closing time. There was a fellow on duty…"

"Cory!" exclaimed Andrea.

"That's the name. He was alone there. He was held up at knife point."

"Ohmigosh! Is he okay?"

"Yes, he's okay. A bit shaken up, but he wasn't hurt."

"Poor Cory," Andrea stammered.

"I didn't realize you knew him," said Jackie.

"I don't. Not really. Justine does."

Andrea could hardly wait to tell Justine. She would have run all the way back to the hoop-and-stick game, but Kenzie was still hurting and limping and making the most of his injury.

Justine was busy supervising a game of ninepins by the time Andrea found her.

"Justine, wait till I tell you!" Andrea called.

"What?"

"Cory was held up at knife point last night at the store!"

"You're kidding!" gasped Justine.

"It's true. I just heard it from Jackie."

"Oh my God! Is he okay?"

"Yes, he is." Andrea relished being the bearer of dramatic news. "It seems that it happened when he was closing the store," she added.

"Did anything get stolen?"

"I don't know. I only heard about it a few minutes ago from Jackie, and she'd just heard it from somebody else," Andrea explained.

"We've got to go there as soon as we can," said Justine urgently.

"Right after work."

CHAPTER TEN ❖

The two girls jumped off the bus and ran all the way to Vivian's store. They were out of breath by the time they charged through the doorway. Vivian was behind the counter, facing a clutch of customers who were listening intently as she described the alarming events of the previous night.

"Cory couldn't say for sure if it was a knife or some other sort of weapon. It was sharp and was pushed into the middle of his back. Poor kid. He must have been terrified," said Vivian sympathetically.

"So then what happened...after he nearly got stabbed?" asked a tall lady in a denim jacket.

"He was forced to open the cash drawer. The thief took all the money, then he forced Cory across the store and shoved him into the cold cupboard. That's where we put the fruit and vegetables at night. The burglar locked him in. The thing is, there's a lock on the outside of that door but normally we never use it. Apparently this fellow was familiar enough with the building and that's why the police suspect he'd been in the store before."

"How long was Cory in the cupboard?" asked Justine anxiously.

"Till nearly midnight. When his parents realized he wasn't home and it was that late, they came looking for him," Vivian replied.

"What's the world coming to?" asked a heavy man in a navy blue T-shirt.

"Makes you wonder," Vivian sighed. "We get quite a few strangers in here in the summertime with all the visitors coming and going from the fortress. There's no way we can remember every single person who shops here."

"Is Cory all right now?" Justine enquired earnestly.

"He's fine, thank God. I told him to take a few days off. What a brave boy. You girls should go over to his house and say hello. I bet he'd appreciate a visit," Vivian suggested.

"His house?" repeated Justine. Somehow she hadn't given any thought to Cory's other life in a house where he presumably lived with his family. All she had ever seen or known of Cory Rankin was right here in this store.

"Good idea," said Andrea enthusiastically, giving Justine a quick jab with her elbow. "Now which is his house? I forget."

"Just up the road there. The yellow one right across from the seniors' home," Vivian gestured.

"Oh, sure. Let's go, Juss," Andrea directed, as she ushered her surprised friend out of the store. They hadn't even had time for a Coke.

At the yellow house they stood looking at the door

for a long minute. It was Andrea who finally knocked. Justine was too nervous to do it.

Someone called, "Come in."

They timidly opened the screen door and found themselves in a large kitchen. Cory was sitting at the kitchen table, along with a lady who surely had to be his mother. When he saw who the visitors were, he looked a bit startled.

"Hi. How's it goin'?" he enquired.

"That's exactly what we came to ask you," laughed Andrea.

"Vivian said we should come over," Justine explained quickly, to justify being so bold as to track Cory right into his home.

He looked perfectly all right. Apart from a piece of masking tape around the bridge of his glasses, no one would have guessed the ordeal he had endured.

"Sit down, girls. I'll put the kettle on for some tea," invited Cory's mother. "You're the girls who stay over at the bed and breakfast, aren't you? And you both work up at the fortress?"

"That's right, Mrs. Rankin. I'm Andrea. This is Justine. We heard about the robbery, so we came over to see if Cory was okay."

"Isn't it dreadful? I can hardly believe it," clucked Mrs. Rankin, who was a small woman with short, dark hair and a round face. She wore baggy blue jeans and a red T-shirt with the words SPORTY FORTY printed on it.

"A robbery right here in Louisbourg. It just proves you don't know who's out there. I never did like the idea of Cory being over at the store late at night. I don't want him working there in the evenings any more; not on his own."

"Aw, Mom," grumbled Cory.

"The police have been here. Twice now," his mother added.

"What did they ask you, Cory?" Justine wanted to know.

"Oh, a lot of things. Did I see the guy's face? What kind of clothes was he wearing? Was he tall or short? What age was he? Had I ever seen the guy in the store before?"

"Had you?"

"No. Trouble was, I didn't really see his face at all. He snuck up behind me while I was putting the oranges and celery and stuff away for the night. He poked something sharp in my back and ordered me to open the cash drawer. He grabbed all the money, then he pushed me across the store so hard it knocked off my glasses. I don't have very good eyesight without them, so all I could say for sure was that he was wearing jeans and sneakers and a baseball cap pulled down around his eyebrows."

"Which sounds like just about every guy in the country," remarked Andrea.

"Did he steal anything else?" asked Justine, eager for every detail.

"All the cigarettes. Fifteen cartons."

"Ewww. Gross," commented Andrea.

"And on top of that he took my Walkman, which was lying on the counter, and that makes me really mad," said Cory angrily.

"Now, Cory, dear, we can get you another," consoled his mother as she got up to make the tea.

It didn't take Justine very long to return to her chatty self once her astonishment at being inside Cory's home wore off. Cory's mother was the sort of woman who made people feel at home, and Cory, despite his recent ordeal, turned out to be a more relaxed person in his own home than he was when he was working at the store.

"So, how do you like Louisbourg?" he asked them both.

"The town or the fortress?" countered Andrea.

"The town."

"Suits me okay," replied Justine.

"Me too," Andrea said with a nod.

"Not much goin' on here," Cory lamented, "unless getting robbed is your idea of a good time."

Both girls giggled a bit and then Justine remarked, "There's not much excitement where I come from either."

"Where's that?"

"River Bourgeois."

"Oh yeah, I've heard of it. But I was never there. They say it's pretty nice."

"It is. Actually…" Justine began, "if you wanted to see it for yourself you could…you could come to my birthday party next week. Andrea's coming too. My brother's coming up to get us so you could get a ride. And you could stay overnight because Marc has space in his room for a camp bed."

"But what would your parents say about that?" asked Mrs. Rankin. "I think you'd better ask them first."

"Oh, my mom and dad wouldn't mind. I'll check first, but I know they like me to bring my friends home. Mom always says we're less likely to get into trouble if we're at home," explained Justine.

"I'm sure she's right," said Mrs. Rankin.

"Mmm," muttered Cory uncertainly. "I dunno if I can go."

"I'm really looking forward to it," said Andrea persuasively.

"Cory, why don't you go too? It would be good for you to get away from all this fuss for a while, to take your mind off the robbery," suggested his mother.

"The robbery's history," declared Cory firmly. There was a long pause before he said anything else. He didn't want anyone to think he had been bothered by what had happened to him…nor that he was going to take his mother's advice. Finally he sighed and shrugged and said, "Might be fun. Why not?"

Justine flashed a wide smile and then, in case she appeared overly enthusiastic, she assumed a matter-of-fact expression and hoped she sounded businesslike.

"Okay. I'll let you know what time my brother's coming. We'd better go now. Thanks for the tea," she said.

"Yes, thanks," added Andrea as they got up to leave.

Justine didn't stop talking all the way back to the Northeast Bed and Breakfast. Andrea had never seen her in such a good mood.

CHAPTER ELEVEN ⚜

"You expect me to play my part in this?" Andrea exclaimed, looking down in mild horror at a slender birch-bark canoe lying half in and half out of the water.

"What's your problem? I thought you said some uncle of yours owned a boat and you loved it," countered Penny as she surveyed the stony shore where the scene would be filmed.

"My uncle has a big scallop-fishing boat. It's got a cabin and an engine, and places to sleep and cook and everything. It's not a bit like this."

"Don't get your shirt in a knot. You won't be in it for long. With any luck we can get the entire shoot done today, as long as the fog hangs around. What's more, we have an experienced paddler among our crew and he's volunteered to teach you how to paddle it. Here he comes now. So get busy and practise. We start work this afternoon."

Penny rushed away and Andrea turned around to see who her instructor would be. Her mouth fell open. Calvin Jefferson Lee was approaching her. Was this her lucky day or what?

"Miss Andrea! Good mawnin'!" he greeted her, lifting

his floppy canvas hat in a mock gesture of southern courtesy, as if he were acting in *Gone with the Wind*. Sometimes Calvin seemed to be coming from another planet. "Back when ah was a student..." he began, as if that part of his life were ancient history. How old was he, anyway? "Ah taught youngsters at a summer camp how to paddle a canoe. So far's ah know nary a one of 'em has drowned. Now then, you watch me real close and heed what ah'm sayin'. You're goin' to catch on real quick 'cause you're smart as a mockin'bird and twice as purty." He winked at her.

Andrea could feel her heart pounding. "I can handle it," she replied bravely, hoping the apprehension wasn't evident in her voice.

Calvin turned out to be a patient teacher. First he demonstrated how to crouch down and grasp both gunnels before setting foot in the canoe. They got in and Calvin paddled away from the shore. Kneeling behind Andrea, he reached around and gently closed a hand over hers as he showed her the correct way to hold the paddle, how to propel the canoe straight ahead, how to turn, and how to stop. His arms felt incredibly strong.

After that he watched from the stern seat while Andrea paddled alone. He reminded her more than once that she must never stand up in a canoe, no matter what. He even described a manoeuvre to get back into the canoe if she happened to fall overboard, but reassured her that that wasn't going to happen as long as she remembered her lessons.

The fog became thicker and for a while they couldn't even see the nearby shore.

"I had the idea they hired stunt people to do scenes like this," Andrea remarked, to let him know she knew a thing or two about making movies.

Calvin gave a quiet, throaty chuckle. "Never fe-ah, dahlin'. The crew's gonna be practically 'longside, just inches away from the sweet sound of your paddle dippin' in the water. Don't you worry that purty li'l head of yours."

There was that word again. Purty.

But Andrea did worry—not about falling overboard and drowning—she was a good swimmer. She was more concerned about making a fool of herself in front of Calvin.

"You're gettin' the hang of it now," he said approvingly. Throughout the lesson he had been facing her back. She wondered if he had merely been watching the way she paddled or if he had actually noticed her. For all she knew he might have been staring off into space. Now Calvin steered the canoe back to the shore, where they got out and together lifted the little craft above the high tide line. The enchanted lesson was over. The fog was lifting a little. Calvin returned to his real work of setting up lighting systems for the film.

Andrea had to return to her real world too. She headed back toward Lartigue House, wishing she could share her excitement with Justine.

Imagine—a whole hour with Calvin! But she knew that if she mentioned her role in the film again, it would send Justine into another long sulk.

Maybe she could phone Suzy, back in Toronto. No, that wasn't possible. Suzy was up north at her parents' summer cottage, where they didn't have a phone. She could phone her mother but that wasn't such a hot idea. How could she tell her mother she had just spent an hour with a guy she wanted to spend all day with? She couldn't. If only there was somebody to share her joy.

Even if Justine had been a willing listener, there wasn't a hope of talking to her that day. In the staff lunch room Justine was now centre stage. Everyone wanted to hear all the details of the robbery at Vivian's store. Andrea was getting a little bored listening to the story over and over, but Justine obviously loved describing it.

"The robber stole mostly the same things—money, cigarettes, and videos," Justine continued knowingly. "And the thing that made Cory so mad was the guy stole his Walkman. Anyway, his grandmother is going to buy him a new stereo on Friday, when she gets her pension cheque."

"How do you know that?" enquired Andrea.

"I know a few things you don't," said Justine smugly.

Penny Goodman appeared at the door of the lunch

room looking for Andrea. "Of all the rotten luck," she grumbled. "The sun is starting to shine. Just when we need the fog, the damn stuff disappears. This afternoon's shoot is cancelled. I'll call you when we need you."

Nothing could have pleased Andrea more. Calvin wouldn't be working either. There might be time for another canoe lesson. Maybe he would even ask her out.

Next morning at seven o'clock there was a phone call for Andrea. "Damnation," she muttered as she hauled herself out of bed and into her bathrobe. "Why does my mother always phone me at this ungodly hour?"

It was Penny Goodman. "Perfect day," she stated. "There's fog everywhere and the forecast says it's going to last. We start the canoe shoot at nine o'clock sharp."

"But I can't work today," Andrea protested. "Today and tomorrow are my days off. I'm going to River Bourgeois with Justine. It's her birthday."

"You've got to work today," Penny insisted. "We're running weeks behind schedule. We've had far too many delays already, what with the weather and everything else. We've got a deadline, you know! This is show business, not a teddy bear's picnic! Do you want this part or not?" she bellowed into the phone. She sounded really angry.

"But…" stammered Andrea.

"I'm sending a car for you in an hour. Make-up first, then I'll meet you on the quay. Don't be late." She hung up.

Andrea went back into the bedroom and sat down heavily on the edge of her bed.

"Happy birthday, Justine. But I can't go with you today," she lamented, tears welling up in her eyes. "I have to stay here and work on that stupid film."

Justine was about to brush her hair but stopped in mid-air. "That's the pits," she grumbled sympathetically. "Everyone at home wants you to come."

"They do?"

"Yeah. And especially my brother Marc. He keeps asking me about you. Anyway, I'll bring you back a piece of birthday cake. Mom always bakes two—one for me and one for Sylvie."

"Thanks a million," said Andrea joylessly. A piece of cake would be nice, but it wasn't going to compensate for this lost opportunity to see Justine in her own home among her family and friends…and to see her brother again.

CHAPTER TWELVE ❖

The Frederic Gate was a huge wooden structure that dominated the waterfront of the fortress. Square and solid, and as tall as a barn, it framed an enormous archway, a replica of the one through which sailors from all over the world had once passed as they unloaded cargoes from sailing ships. It had been the commercial centre of this community, a gathering place for colonists eager for news from the rest of the world.

Nothing significant happened here now, but tourists liked to have their photographs taken standing in front of it. Andrea had memorized the facts about this imposing landmark so that she could answer questions when visitors asked. However, today she didn't want to talk to anyone; she thought she was going to cry. Justine and Cory had already left for a fun weekend in River Bourgeois. Andrea was still uncertain about her ability to paddle that wobbly canoe on her own. Calvin had not volunteered to give her a second lesson yesterday, and today he was nowhere to be seen. Several other crew members were there, setting up their equipment, but not him. Didn't they need a gaffer today? Where was he?

Grumpy Grundy came striding out of the fog towards her, waving a friendly greeting. He seemed to be in an uncharacteristically good mood. "Yon rising star appeareth," he proclaimed as if he were on a stage.

"She braveth the winds of change
And the tide of time,
Her secret held against her gentle breast
And courageous heart."

What's with this guy? Andrea wondered. He's the director, but he acts like a frustrated actor. What was he rambling on about anyway? The secret note, which was the reason—in the film—that she was making this canoe trip, was in the pocket of her skirt and not against her… honestly, what an idiot.

"I want to see a smile on that pretty face," he continued, this time in his normal voice. "Just think, ah, Adriana, you could be nominated for Best Supporting Actress for this role. Stranger things have happened. You're a talented young lady, you…"

"My name is Andrea!" she almost shouted.

"So it is. Let's get to work. We'll begin with you paddling away from us, glancing back once or twice with your dark, anxious look. You're concerned that someone may be following you."

"The cameraman will be, that's for sure," Andrea muttered under her breath.

"After that," he instructed, "keep on paddling out towards the centre of the bay. We'll do a second shoot there, only from a launch instead of the shore. And remember, if you feel uneasy about anything just give us a shout."

"I'll do that," said Andrea coolly.

Charlene appeared with her portable make-up kit. She dabbed more powder on Andrea's face, aimed hair spray on her bangs, and twisted a few curls with a butane curling iron.

"What's the matter with you today, honey?" she asked. "You look like you've lost your last friend."

"I probably have," Andrea agreed gloomily.

"I don't believe it. You cheer up now, you hear? This film's nearly done. I want outta here as much as you do."

"All I wanted was my two days off to go to River Bourgeois."

"Where?"

"Where Justine lives. You remember her. We did a scene together in the governor's drawing room."

"Now don't you fret. There's gonna be other times to visit with your friends. You got your whole life ahead of you."

"If I haven't screwed it up," Andrea lamented.

Charlene merely smiled.

"We haven't got all day!" shouted Grumpy Grundy from the water's edge, where he was holding the canoe in place with his foot. Andrea grasped the gunnels, placed one foot in the middle of the canoe, and with the other shoved it away from the shore. It was tricky to manoeuvre her way into a canoe when she was wearing a long skirt. Cautiously she settled into the stern seat and slowly paddled away. She soon discovered that it wasn't as easy to keep the canoe moving in a straight line this time. The tide was going out and the current tended to pull the canoe to the left. She paddled hard to the right and, after every third or fourth stroke, looked back through the foggy murk towards the camera with her much-practised expression of anxiety. Finally she heard the welcome word "Cut!"

"Stay there, Andrea," called Penny.

Andrea sat very still in the canoe in the fog. The sound of voices carried clearly in this kind of weather, and she could hear the crew talking among themselves as they loaded film equipment into a motor launch. After a while she heard the motor start. They were heading her way.

The thing about fog is that it doesn't stay still for long. Today, it wafted back and forth across the bay. One minute Andrea could see the shore and the next minute she couldn't.

"As long as it doesn't blow away altogether," Andrea prayed, because if it did she would have to do this scene over again another day.

The launch with the crew and cameras pulled up beside her.

"Okay, brave little courier," ordered Penny, "now we want to see you paddling purposefully in the direction of the lighthouse."

"But I can't see the lighthouse. The fog's too thick," Andrea complained.

"Of course you can't see the lighthouse and we don't want to either. It hadn't been built in the eighteenth century, remember? Just paddle in that direction."

Andrea paddled diligently into the grey and blurry distance. Stroke. Stroke. Stroke. Another stroke. Then a backward glance. More strokes. More backward glances. Surely she had paddled and glanced backward long enough by now.

"I am royally fed up," Andrea muttered through clenched teeth. "I have had enough. I am—"

Abruptly she realized that the engine in the launch had stopped and the crew might be able to hear her. She turned around to see what was happening. Had they changed their minds again? She could see only a dark blur in the fog where the boat ought to be.

"Andrea! Can you hear me?" came the distant voice of Penny Goodman.

"I hear you," yelled Andrea.

"Something's wrong with this blasted engine. Better come over here till we get it fixed!" Andrea dipped the paddle in the water and started to steer the canoe in a wide arc. She soon realized she had pulled too far to the right, so she switched the paddle to the other side and stroked hard to the left.

"Dammit," she muttered. Now she was too far to the left. She switched the paddle again, trying to remember something in Calvin's instructions about a "J" stroke. What had he said? Turning a canoe around was not as easy as it looked. She switched to the other side again and then—oops!—the paddle slipped right out of her hands and was floating away from the canoe!

She bent over and reached out to grab it, stretching her fingers to the limit, but the infuriating paddle floated away from her. She leaned out farther…just a little more…a little more…and then had to pull back a split second before the canoe would have overturned.

How humiliating! She turned to see if anyone was watching her, but the launch had completely disappeared into the fog.

Now what? The launch was back there somewhere and for a moment Andrea considered jumping overboard and swimming towards it. She was confident about her ability to swim, but how far away were they anyway? And of course she was wearing her costume! Maybe, if she took off her cape and chemise and skirt, she could jump in wearing only her bra and panties. She decided against that. It would be altogether too embarrassing to be seen by the whole crew in her underwear. Besides, the water was awfully cold, even though it was August. What if she got a cramp? She would drown for sure, because no one could see where she was. A shiver ran down her spine as the paddle drifted out of sight into the mist.

"Aaandreeeaah!" The voice sounded a hundred miles away. "Where aaaaaare yooooou?"

"Heeeeere!"

"Stay there. We're…fix…engine…" The voice died away into the clammy silence.

"Okaaaaay!" hollered Andrea. There was absolutely nothing else she could do. She was so angry at her own clumsiness. What was Calvin going to think when he heard about this? His pupil had failed. She felt so helpless and so silly and she couldn't stop shivering. She clutched her woollen cape tightly around her shoulders. What a ridiculous predicament this was. There was nothing to do and nothing to look at even. It was just as well she didn't realize the tide was gradually carrying the canoe out to sea.

Andrea began to wonder what time it was. She had had to leave her wrist-watch behind because, in the era of the film, watches had yet to be invented. It felt as if she had been drifting in the canoe for hours.

There was only one distraction—the seagulls. Every once in a while a gull glided by like a ghost.

She had never taken much notice of these common-place birds before. They had always been just part of the scenery. Now they were company. She began counting every gull, a game she used to play with her mother whenever they made a long car journey and counted the number of cows they saw, or horses, or barns, or red cars. It made the time pass more quickly. One gull, two gulls, three gulls, four…After a while—and she had no idea how long—she was up to sixteen. She also noticed for the first time that some gulls had black backs and grey fronts and some had white fronts and grey backs. Were they different species altogether? Next time she was near a library she would go in and ask for a book about birds and find out. Then she began to wonder if she ever would be in a library again.

It slowly dawned on her that a really long time had gone by. Where on earth was she—no, not on the earth, on the ocean? Where was everyone else? Had they gone ashore and abandoned her? What would her mother do when her only daughter didn't come home? Would she be angry at Andrea's stupidity? No, she would be heartbroken.

"Oh, why did I want this dumb job anyway?" Andrea sobbed, tears streaming down her face. "I wish I wasn't here. I wish I was at Justine's party." She wept until the whole canoe shook.

The fog was growing thicker. Then finally she heard something besides the screeching of the gulls. It was a motor, but one with an entirely different sound from the launch carrying the film crew. Now she was really afraid. Whoever was driving this motor boat didn't know she was out here. They wouldn't be able to see her until they got very close, and they might easily smash into the canoe and break it into splinters. She could be hurled into the ocean, bleeding and possibly unconscious.

She sat bolt upright, uncertain what to do. Maybe she should scream, but if she did would anyone hear her? If she stood up and waved her arms she would be more visible. But no, she remembered she must never stand up in a canoe. Those were Calvin's ironbound instructions.

The sound of the engine had become a deep, sullen roar. Andrea crouched down in the canoe, gripping the gunnels so hard her hands were turning white. But what was the point of that? It would be better to shout and scream. There was a remote chance someone might hear her.

"Hey! I'm over here!" she hollered into the grey distance. "Here I am!" she screamed, sitting bolt upright, waving her cape. If only the cape hadn't been brown. If it was yellow or red the people in the boat might notice something before they smashed into her. "I'm over here!" she screeched, her throat hurting from the effort. But she could still hear the boat heading towards her.

Then, all of a sudden, the threatening roar stopped, diminishing to a low purr. Staring into the fog, Andrea saw a dim shape beginning to emerge. It grew larger until she could see the bow of a boat as big as her uncle's inching through the murk towards her.

Someone had seen her! She resisted the urge to jump to her feet, but the tears began again. This time they were tears of joy. Moments later a big grey boat slowed to a stop alongside the canoe and a smiling face looked out of the wheelhouse window.

"Hi there, young lady. Need a ride?"

CHAPTER THIRTEEN ❖

A broad-shouldered Mountie held a coiled rope in his
hands. He hurled it towards Andrea, and she grabbed it.
He pulled the canoe alongside and tied it securely to his
boat, then he reached out a hand to help Andrea climb
aboard.

"You okay? I've got blankets on board, and a first-aid
kit, and food and water," he offered. He wore a badge on
his shirt that said D. Orzechowski.

"I am absolutely fine, thanks," insisted Andrea shakily.

A flicker of a smile crossed the Mountie's face, then
he started the engine. "So, looks as if you were up the
creek without a paddle, eh?"

"It's not a creek. It's an ocean. The paddle slipped out
of my hands when I was switching sides. I tried and tried
to reach it, but it kept floating away. I was so darn mad,"
Andrea admitted.

"So that's what happened. Your pals were sure
worried about you. They couldn't get their engine going,
and they didn't have a clue where you'd got to. That's
when they called us. How long were you out here?"

"I don't know. It felt like forever."

"Were you scared?"

"No. Well, maybe. Just a bit."

"Luckily our radar picked you up. The tide had carried you a fair distance out of the harbour. Bet you didn't want to spend the night out there, did you?"

"No."

"And where is your life jacket, young lady? There are water safety rules, as I am sure you are aware."

"I couldn't carry one because they hadn't been invented in the eighteenth century," Andrea explained.

He glanced at her with a puzzled expression. "What kind of an excuse is that? That was then and this is now."

"You don't understand. We were filming. I'm in a movie. It was a scene where I had to paddle across the bay carrying an important secret letter in my pocket. I had to paddle and paddle and keep looking back anxiously to make sure no one had seen me," Andrea continued.

"They sure in heck wouldn't. Not in this fog."

"A life jacket would have looked all wrong historically. The film has to appear authentic," Andrea stated emphatically.

"Yeah, but they didn't have movie cameras back in those days either, did they?"

"Well, no," Andrea conceded. This guy was missing the point. Historic films weren't about cameras; they were about history.

"Guess that explains why you're not exactly dressed for canoeing in the North Atlantic."

Andrea had forgotten how incongruous she must have looked, sitting in a canoe dressed in a long-sleeved white shirt, a bonnet, an ankle-length skirt, and a woollen cape, all soaked by the fog. She took off her bonnet and then ran her hand lightly across her cheek, suddenly conscious of the make-up she was wearing. She was worried that the mascara had started to run while she had been crying.

"So, I've rescued a movie star, have I?" enquired the constable, one eye on her and the other on his radar screen.

"I'm not a star. I don't speak one word in this film. I'm supposed to be a lady's maid," Andrea said, a little apologetically.

"You've got to start somewhere. Maybe next time you'll get a bigger role," he consoled her.

"I don't think so. I don't like the film business all that much. What I'm really doing is working at the Fortress of Louisbourg for the summer. It was just a fluke that I was asked to play a role in this film."

By this time they could see the misty outline of the shore. In a few more minutes the Mountie cut the engine and eased the boat alongside Louisbourg's public wharf, where a crowd had gathered. When they saw Andrea standing beside the policeman people began to cheer. Andrea climbed up on the dock and Penny Goodman rushed towards her and surprised her with a hug. Jackie Cormier was there too and she gave Andrea an even bigger hug. Even Grumpy Grundy patted her shoulder and actually smiled at her for the first time since she had met him.

"Spot of bad luck," he said kindly, "but all's well that ends well."

"Honestly, I was fine. I lost the paddle, that's all," Andrea shrugged, trying to make light of her ordeal. She was embarrassed at all the fuss, although she was glad they cared. People had worried about her, but she was ashamed that she hadn't handled the canoe properly. She looked around to see if Calvin was there, but fortunately, this time, he wasn't.

"I'll be on my way then," said Constable Orzechowski.

"Thanks a lot for rescuing me," said Andrea, amid a chorus of gratitude from everyone else.

"All in a day's work."

Jackie Cormier offered Andrea a ride back to town. Andrea climbed into her car and for a long time didn't say a thing. She felt she had ruined everything—her final scene in the canoe, the chance to attend Justine's party, and, even worse, a chance to impress Calvin by showing that she was one heck of a paddler. She wasn't. Nothing had worked out the way she had hoped.

"You weren't frightened, were you, Andrea?" asked Jackie.

"Nope. Just mad at myself."

"I know the feeling," Jackie sympathized. "I didn't realize what had happened. I was simply driving by...

on my way back from visiting Mom in Sydney. I could see all these film people gathered together down at the wharf, so I parked and got out, curious to find out what was going on. That was when someone told me. You were adrift somewhere in a canoe and they had called an RCMP rescue unit to find you…they hoped! Luckily, they had just got news that you were on board the police boat and you would be there soon. What a relief!"

"No big deal," Andrea shrugged. "It's not as if there was a terrible storm or anything. The ocean was as calm as a cup of tea. It was…boring, that's all. But it was starting to get kind of cold out there."

"I'll bet."

Andrea didn't want to talk about it any more. She wanted to forget the whole episode, and she hoped everyone else would too. She just stared out the window. Then her eye caught the name on an envelope on the dashboard of the car. It was addressed to Mrs. John A. MacDonald.

"Hey, how about that?" Andrea asked brightly. "A letter for the wife of the first prime minister of Canada."

"What?"

"It says 'Mrs. John A. MacDonald.'"

"Oh," laughed Jackie. "That's my mom. I have to deal with her mail. It's one of those government forms that have to be filled out."

"Your name used to be MacDonald? So you're not

French then," Andrea remarked. "I just assumed you were. Jacqueline Cormier. It sounds…well…French."

"Who knows what anyone is, really? I was named Jacqueline after my dad. He was John Alan MacDonald, but everyone knew him as Jack."

"Maybe you're distantly related to Sir John A. Macdonald."

Jackie chuckled. "I don't think so."

"I guess there are a lot of MacDonalds all over the place."

"Tell me about it," said Jackie. "The MacDonald clan wouldn't dare hold a reunion. There isn't a building big enough in the world to hold us all. Did you ever look at the Sydney-Glace Bay phone book? You've never seen so many MacDonalds. And it's the same in a lot of places across Canada."

Andrea returned to her room. She felt depressed. It was Saturday night and she was alone and she didn't have anything to do. She thought she might phone somebody, but she got as far as the telephone in the hall and was too discouraged to pick it up. Idly, she leafed through the phone book and, sure enough, there were three full pages of people whose last name was MacDonald, or McDonald. Forty-one of them bore the first name John.

As she stood there the phone rang. It was Justine.

"Hi, Juss! How's your birthday party?" Andrea asked wistfully.

"Fab-u-luss! Lots of kids are here. Mom and Dad gave me new sneakers for my birthday. Sylvie got some too, of course. So what have you been up to?"

"Actually, quite a lot. I'll tell you about it sometime," replied Andrea.

"Hang on a minute. Marc wants to talk to you."

There was a pause, then Justine's brother spoke. "How's it goin'? Too bad you missed the party."

"Sure is. Wish I was there."

"I was just thinkin'…"

"What?"

"I'm comin' up tomorrow to drive Justine and Cory back."

"Uh huh."

"Maybe I'll see ya when I get there?"

"Well…okay. If you bring some of that birthday cake…then we could go out for some pop or something."

"Sounds good to me. See ya then."

"See ya," echoed Andrea, hoping she sounded as cool as the Atlantic fog. The truth was she suddenly felt as bright as sunshine. She was delighted. Marc was obviously a quiet guy…but…maybe quiet guys were all right. Tomorrow she would find out.

CHAPTER FOURTEEN ⚜

The next day the film crew began packing up. The
shoot was finally complete. Men and women were busy
dismantling lights, coiling cables, and hauling crates of
equipment towards a fleet of trucks parked near the bus
depot.

Andrea had decided not to take the day off after all.
She didn't feel like spending it alone. She kept an eye on
the film crew from time to time, wondering if Calvin
might appear. Where had he been, anyway, during her
ordeal on the water? Had what happened to her—as
well as what might have happened—mattered to him at
all? Did he care if she was alive or dead? "Filmmakers,"
she thought bitterly, "who needs them anyway?" She
switched her thoughts to Marc Marchand, whom she
would meet later that day. He sounded a whole lot nicer.

She was glad to be back at her regular job. There was
something reassuring about the routine of shepherding
the children around, organizing games, and chatting
with the tourists. From now on, no one was going to
make her spend her time running down some stupid
hill or paddling around in a fog. When she happened
to see Penny Goodman in the distance marching along

purposefully, Andrea felt relieved to know she would no longer have to take orders from her. It crossed her mind that Penny might know where Calvin was today…but, no, she wasn't going to ask.

Penny spotted her. "Andrea! Just the person I was looking for. You've got a surprise visitor. Up in the visitors' rest building."

"Is that so?" Andrea replied, trying to sound as calm as she could. So, Marc Marchand had arrived, and quite a bit earlier than she had expected.

"I've just come from there," added Penny. "I think you should hurry over right away."

"Okay," Andrea agreed.

"And, by the way, thank you, Andrea," said Penny. "You've been a trouper. Who knows, maybe the next time we're working on a film up here in Canada we'll call on you again."

"Maybe," Andrea muttered as she turned and headed up the road. Yeah, Penny, maybe lots of things. Maybe life would be normal again. Maybe Justine would give up sulking. Maybe there would be another chance to visit River Bourgeois. Maybe Marc would turn out to be… She suddenly felt so light-hearted that she abandoned her dignity and ran the final block towards the building. She stopped long enough outside the door to smooth her hair and make sure her bonnet was in place, then she strode in. She was totally unprepared for what she found. There stood her mother.

"Mom!"

"Sweetie!" she cried and held out her arms to give her astonished daughter a hug.

"Mom. What…I didn't know you were coming," Andrea gasped.

"Surprise, surprise! I finished teaching my course and…I don't know…I just felt it was the right time for a little trip. There was an airline seat sale…so here I am."

Andrea didn't know what to say. The surprise of discovering her mother here in the fortress left her speechless. Finally she managed to ask, "How did you get in? How did you find me?"

"Easy enough. I just bought a ticket like any other tourist. I wasn't sure how I was going to find you actually, until I noticed a woman carrying a clipboard. She looked as if she worked here, so I simply asked her if she knew you. And she did. She said she'd keep an eye out for you. Is she your boss?"

"No, that's Penny. She's part of the film crew. She's not my boss, I like my boss. Penny's sort of…well, she'll be leaving soon. How long are you going to stay, Mom?"

"A little while. I've got a room at the Foxberry Inn. It's quite nice. But I'll tell you what would be even nicer—why don't I take you to lunch? I made some enquiries and they recommended Hôtel de la Marine, right here in the fortress. Apparently you have to eat the sort of food they ate two hundred and something years ago. Sounds like fun. Have you tried it?"

"Gosh no. We bring sandwiches and eat in the employees' lunchroom. I'm not sure if I'm allowed to eat in any of the restaurants here."

"Could you ask someone for permission?"

"I guess I could phone the office."

Andrea called Jackie Cormier and explained that her mother had arrived out of the blue and asked if the two of them could have lunch together in a fortress restaurant.

"That's a happy surprise," exclaimed Jackie. "Actually, staff members aren't supposed to eat there, but we'll make an exception. Attendance is low today, so I'm sure there'll be room. I'd like to meet your mother. If I have any spare time I'll drop by and say hello."

At Hôtel de la Marine the diners sat on backless stools at wooden tables covered with white tablecloths made of coarse linen. They were served a hearty soup in wide bowls that were reproductions of the pottery that had been used there in 1744. Andrea's mother ordered a glass of wine, which came in a thick, green-tinted glass. The waitresses wore the same kind of clothes as Andrea: long, dark skirts with pale aprons, and white shirts and bonnets. The smiling woman who served them was about the same age as Andrea's mother. She greeted Andrea like an old friend.

"Sounds like you had quite a time of it yesterday," she remarked.

"Oh, that," shrugged Andrea. It hadn't occurred to her

that everyone who worked at the fortress would have heard about her escapade in the canoe and her rescue by the police. News travels fast.

"What happened yesterday?" asked her mother.

"Oh, nothing much. This is my mother." Andrea turned and introduced her to the waitress. "She just got here, all the way from Toronto."

"Is that right? You must be really pleased to see your daughter."

"I certainly am."

Andrea didn't want her mother to find out she had been stranded in a canoe in the fog and had had to be rescued. Her mother was always worrying about dreadful things happening anyway. The waitress was about to add something, but Andrea interrupted her by asking questions about the soup and how it was made, anything to change the subject until this too-friendly woman would go away.

"What did happen to you yesterday?" her mother asked for the second time, once the waitress had left.

"Um...remember I told you I was playing a part, a very small part, in a film."

"I remember."

"Well, we did the final shoot yesterday. I had to paddle a canoe and—silly me—the paddle slipped out of my hands. They had to come and get me. No big deal."

Her mother looked alarmed.

"I was only out here in the harbour. There's no way

you can get lost or blown away or anything," Andrea insisted.

"That would depend," said her mother sternly, "on the visibility, the direction of the wind, and the tide. I know about these things. I'm from Newfoundland, remember?"

"Yes, Mom, I remember. Anyway, the filming is over. I won't be playing any more roles."

"Imagine, my daughter in a movie! I can hardly wait to see it. Was it fun?"

"Well, at times it was. The first day they put all that make-up on us and we hardly recognized ourselves in the mirror. That was wild. And then they coached us on what expressions to use so we would look as if we were eavesdropping. That was something else because that's the reason they noticed us in the first place. We really were trying to listen in."

"What was the story all about?"

"Actually, it was sort of stupid. It's some kind of love story. The guy who played the lead was a jerk. The director was always in a bad mood. Penny, his assistant—the one you met—was always bugging me about something. It took forever to get anything done. I enjoyed it, but I don't think I want a career in film."

"You do know that nothing gets accomplished without effort. These people obviously had a lot of work to organize. It can't have been easy for them." Her mother took a sip of her wine.

Andrea glanced past her mother's shoulder to see two people coming through the doorway of the restaurant. One was Calvin Jefferson Lee, and right beside him, holding his hand, was smiling, gorgeous Deborah Cluett, minus the monstrous wig and the lavish clothes. She wore pale blue jeans and a clingy white T-shirt. Her blond hair was short and windblown. She looked a lot younger and a lot prettier than when she had been made-up and dressed for the film.

"Andrea, what is it? You look as if you've seen a ghost," said her mother, turning around to see what was behind her.

Andrea couldn't take her eyes off the pair as they were ushered to a table on the other side of the room. Calvin and Deborah! Was this their first date? It didn't appear to be. They were sharing a laugh about something and looking directly into each other's eyes. How long had this been going on? Andrea felt as if she'd been hit by a truck. Would they notice her? she wondered. What would be worse: to be seen there, with her mother of all people, or not to be noticed at all?

"It's nothing, Mom. Just some people I know. They're eating here too." Her mother leaned towards her, suddenly looking very serious.

"Andrea," she began in a solemn tone. "I have something I want to tell you. Something very important."

"I know, Mom. Perseverance and patience. I realize

how hard all those people had to work to get the movie made. I know about putting one hundred per cent into whatever I do. You've told me before." Andrea sighed.

"No, not that, sweetie, though I'm glad you remember. I have something else on my mind. And it's not altogether easy for me to say it."

Andrea stopped staring at Calvin and Deborah long enough to catch the look on her mother's face. This was no pep talk about getting things done. It dawned on her that something awful might be happening. What?

"Mom," she began cautiously, "are you and Brad splitting up?"

Her mother burst into a brief laugh but quickly returned to the earnestness of a moment earlier. "No, no, no. Brad and I are just fine. And he sends you his love. You mean a lot to him. I know it has been an adjustment for you...trying to accept a stepfather. But don't worry, Brad and I plan to stay together. Did I tell you Brad put up that new wallpaper you wanted in your room?"

"He did?" Andrea brightened.

"He sure did. But this isn't what I want to talk about right now. I want to tell you something that you might not—"

"Well, would you look who's he-ah!" called Calvin in a loud, you-all drawl that could be heard right across the restaurant.

Andrea blushed. He finally had noticed her. "Hi," responded Andrea weakly, waving the fingers of her right hand.

Calvin and Deborah got up and came over. "This's a pleasure," said Calvin warmly. "Ah was sayin' to Debbie how ah hoped we'd get a chance to say goodbye to you 'fore we left."

So he called her Debbie, did he? Andrea swallowed and tried not to show her feelings. "I guess you're outta here soon, eh?" she said.

"Tomorrow morning." Debbie smiled, looking relieved.

"Um...this is my mother," Andrea explained reluctantly.

Her mother smiled and shook hands with them. There was an exchange of friendly greetings. Where are you from? How long are you staying? What a lovely daughter you have!

Andrea felt diminished, as if she had turned into a little girl again, stranded in the midst of a bunch of people talking over her head. They seemed so old. How old was Deborah anyway? She had heard that Calvin was supposed to be about twenty, but Deborah—Debbie— had to be older than that. She was too old for Calvin. But what did it matter to Andrea? They were probably an item. They were leaving Louisbourg, leaving Canada, leaving her behind.

"I like your friends," her mother remarked after

Calvin and Deborah had returned to their table.

"Not friends exactly. We worked together on the film. They're okay," Andrea admitted grudgingly.

"I suppose you've made quite a few friends here?"

"A few."

"And maybe a boyfriend?"

"Not really."

"No?"

"No."

"Now then, Andrea. As I started to say, there's something I've been meaning to tell you…"

Just at this moment the cheery waitress returned with the rest of their meal and plonked down two heavy plates laden with a mixture of boiled cabbage and turnips and small chunks of beef.

"Bon appetit!" She smiled, busying herself clearing the plates and the crumbs from the table beside them.

"I'd call this a Jigg's dinner," remarked Andrea's mother.

"It's supposed to be French, Mom."

"Call it what you like. We ate it in Newfoundland too. This is what I grew up on."

As long as the waitress remained within earshot, Andrea's mother made no further attempt at disclosing whatever it was she wanted to tell her daughter. Andrea sensed it was bad news of some kind, and she didn't want to hear it. Not now. She had had enough bad news for one day: Calvin and Deborah. How come she hadn't heard about them before? Every once in a while she shot a furtive glance at the couple on the far side of the room, looking at one another with those lovey-dovey eyes, those happy smiles, and the shared laughs.

"Sorry, we're full right now," she heard the waitress say to someone at the door.

"If you'll wait in the hallway, it shouldn't be too long."

"I've only come to deliver a message." Andrea recognized Justine's voice. "And there she is, right over there."

"Oh, Juss."

"I'm sorry to interrupt your meal, Andrea, but…"

"That's okay. This is my mother. Mom, this is my roommate, Justine."

"Hello," said Justine hurriedly. "Jackie told me where you were. There's someone waiting to see you, like, right now. It's Marc," Justine continued breathlessly.

"Who's Marc?" asked her mother.

"Marc's my brother," explained Justine. "He's outside. He just wants to say hi to Andrea. He was hoping to stay for a while, but it turns out he has to go back right away."

"Oh. Too bad," said Andrea, trying not to sound crestfallen as she got up from her chair.

"I hope you won't be gone long," cautioned her mother.

"Not a chance," said Andrea glumly.

Marc Marchand was in front of the restaurant, shuffling his feet on the dusty surface of the road. When he saw Andrea, he held out a plastic supermarket bag with a small package in it. "Here's your piece of cake. Hope you like chocolate," he offered.

"Sure. Thanks," Andrea replied without enthusiasm. She didn't give a hoot about the birthday cake. It had only been an excuse to get together but evidently that wasn't going to happen now.

"I have to get back home or else my dad's gonna kill me," said Marc half-jokingly.

"Why is that?"

"Because of the scallops."

"The scallops?"

"Yeah. See, we're starting a scallop farm and the first couple of years it takes a lot of work, and right now is the season when we all pitch in and help," he explained.

"A farm for scallops," Andrea mused. She could only remember Justine talking about cows and pigs. "I thought they caught scallops in the ocean."

"Oh, sure they do. But that's doing it the hard way. This new way they grow in cages made of net, deep down in the water. You can bring in a lot more of them…eventually."

"No kidding," remarked Andrea, trying to sound interested, even though she didn't really understand what he was talking about.

"So, um, enjoy your cake…"

"Sure."

"And...Justine was saying that maybe when you're finished working here, at the end of summer, maybe you'll come home then...with her...for a visit."

"Sounds neat. I can meet your dog and all those hens and cows. And see those scallops running around the farm," she quipped.

Marc laughed. He seemed to like her sense of humour. "Shellfish don't run. But I'd better. See ya."

"See ya," Andrea repeated as she turned to go back into the restaurant. In her absence Justine had occupied her empty chair. She and her mother were chatting away like old friends. Justine, Andrea figured, was probably telling her mother the story of her life. Whatever she was saying, it was making her mother smile. Her frown had disappeared and she looked as if she was enjoying herself. The bad news she was planning to tell Andrea would obviously have to wait.

CHAPTER FIFTEEN ✤

That evening Andrea and her mother ate their supper in a little café next door to the inn. There were only three other customers, and her mother had deliberately chosen a table near the back, as far away from the other people as they could sit. They both ordered cheeseburgers and fries.

Andrea concentrated on making her meal last as long as possible, hoping to delay the inevitable. What was her mother going to tell her? Did they have to move again? That would be a royal pain, now that she had finally made some friends at her new school. Maybe her mother had lost her job. Maybe Brad had lost his. Were they going to be poor and hungry? Maybe it was even worse than that. Maybe her mother had been diagnosed with a fatal disease. She didn't look sick. She just looked very, very serious.

"Andrea, do you remember me telling you that I worked in a fish-packing plant a long time ago?"

"Sure, Mom, I remember," Andrea replied, a bit wearily. Why did her mother want to reminisce about that? What more could she say about packing fish except that it had been a cold place to work, and hard on her hands and feet? Andrea had heard all this before.

"I never told you where it was, did I?"

Andrea thought about it for a moment. She had never heard the name of the place. It hardly mattered. She shook her head.

"It was in North Sydney," said her mother.

Andrea looked up, only a bit surprised. Her mother came from Anderson's Arm, Newfoundland. But everyone knew Newfoundlanders sometimes had to go elsewhere to work. That was the way things were.

"I stayed over here for a year or so. It wasn't the best year of my life, as I think I've told you. I wasn't much older than you are now. When it was all over, I went back home to Anderson's Arm. I returned to high school and a year later I graduated. I've never regretted that."

"I know, Mom," nodded Andrea. She had heard that piece of advice before too. Maybe a hundred times.

"But there's one thing I've never told you, and I'm going to tell you now," her mother continued, taking a deep breath and twisting her napkin.

Andrea looked at her mother's face apprehensively. "What?" she dared to ask.

"I...I had a baby...that year," her mother said, getting the words out with difficulty.

"What?" blurted Andrea.

"It's true. A baby girl was born to me shortly before I returned home to Newfoundland. I...I gave her up for

adoption. There just wasn't any other choice…for me…
then."

Andrea was dumbfounded. She couldn't think of
anything appropriate to say. What does someone say
when struck by a thunderbolt? Her mother had had a
baby when she was, what, sixteen or seventeen years old.
Why was she telling her about it now? That baby would
be a grown-up person now. That baby…that woman…
Andrea suddenly realized, would be her half-sister. A
sister! She had always wanted a sister. Somewhere—out
there in the world—she had one. It was all too much!
She began to laugh uncontrollably. Then she choked and
almost cried, while her mother sat across the table from
her, biting her lower lip and looking guilty.

"Andrea, I…"

"Mom. Mom," Andrea hiccuped. "It's okay, really. You
just told me I've got a sister. It isn't funny, I know, but…
somehow…it is kind of amazing. I always wanted a sister.
I mean, I'll never know her, but just the idea of it…"

"I hope you're not angry," said her mother in an
uncertain voice.

"No way, Mom. Why would I be? I'm glad you finally
told me. And I'll tell you something. You can trust me, I
won't tell a soul," Andrea promised.

"It doesn't have to be a secret any more."

"Really? Does Brad know?" Andrea asked.

"Yes, I've told him. He doesn't have a problem with
it."

Andrea thought about that for a minute. Was everyone going to know about this? Was this a good idea? "Did my father know?" she asked.

"No. Albert didn't know. I didn't tell him. There didn't seem to be any reason to talk about it. We had you. We were a happy family. But, as the years go by, things change. You see…I now know where my first daughter is. I know her name. I came here to find her. She lives right here in Louisbourg."

"Here? Oh my gawww…"

"I know. It really is incredible. That's why, when I heard you were coming here to work, I was, well, uncomfortable. I didn't like the idea of you coming to Cape Breton Island on your own, because of what had happened to me."

"Oh, Mom." Andrea sighed.

"You see, I had applied to an agency to try find my lost child a couple of years ago. You can make contact only if both the mother and the child make an application. It's been just a few months since she applied too, and I discovered where she lived. The name of this place has been in my mind so much."

"What's her name?" asked Andrea, suddenly curious.

"Eleanor."

Andrea repeated the name. Eleanor. My sister, Eleanor. Somehow she couldn't suppress more laughter, even though this wasn't funny either. Right here in this town she had a real, live sister named Eleanor. "What's her last name?"

"MacDonald."

"Oh, Mom!" cried Andrea, convulsed with untimely mirth. "You won't believe how many people there are around here named MacDonald. There are thousands of them, columns and columns in the phone book. How on earth are you going to find Eleanor MacDonald?"

"Actually, that was the name of the family who adopted her. She has since been married, and she goes by her husband's name."

"What's that?"

"Cormier. Her full name is Eleanor Jacqueline MacDonald Cormier. And I intend to find her."

Andrea gasped and clapped her hand over her mouth. For the longest time she couldn't utter a word.

CHAPTER SIXTEEN ⚜

"Andrea! This is a nice surprise. Come on in," invited Jackie Cormier hospitably. "I was just putting Kenzie to bed. It's story time, and you know how kids are about their bedtime stories. Make yourself at home, and I'll be with you shortly."

Andrea entered the kitchen uneasily and sat on the edge of a chair. She could feel her heart pounding as she rehearsed in her mind what she had come to tell Jackie. This had to be the most intense experience of her life, and probably it soon would be the same for Jackie too. How do you tell someone this kind of news?

It had fallen to Andrea to do it when her mother totally lost her cool after Andrea explained that she and Jackie Cormier had been working together all summer.

"Break the ice for me. Please," her mother had asked. "You already know her and I don't. I'm scared. What if it turns out she hates me because I had to give her up?"

"All right," Andrea agreed soothingly, confident that Jackie would be truly happy to finally meet her birth mother. But now, sitting in this friendly kitchen, she wasn't quite so sure.

She could hear Jackie's voice reading to her son. It must have been amusing because every now and then Kenzie burst out laughing. Kenzie, she suddenly realized, was related to her too. She was—what—his aunt? His half-aunt? Aunt Andrea.

The story lasted about five more minutes. For Andrea, it seemed like five hours. Finally Jackie tiptoed down the darkened hall and emerged into the bright kitchen.

"I would have thought you and your mother might be out seeing the sights somewhere tonight," Jackie said.

"No," replied Andrea solemnly.

"Can I make you a cup of tea?" offered Jackie.

"I have to talk to you, Jackie. It's pretty serious."

Jackie immediately sat down across the table and gave Andrea her full attention.

"Is something wrong?" she asked earnestly.

"Nothing's wrong. And this is not about me. It's about you."

"Me?"

"Jackie, I need to know something."

"What?"

"Is your full name Eleanor Jacqueline?" asked Andrea, trying to quell the tremor in her voice.

"Yes," Jackie nodded, looking perplexed.

"And you did tell me you were a MacDonald before you got married?"

"Yes," replied Jackie, wondering why any of this mattered to Andrea.

"Then I'll just come right out and say it," said Andrea, clearing her throat. "Jackie, you know how you are adopted?"

Jackie leaned back and started to giggle, relieved that she wasn't about to hear some disturbing news. Finally she stopped and said, "Oh, Andrea, I am sorry. I didn't mean to make light of what you told me. It's just that... of course I know I'm adopted. I've always known that. My parents married late in life. They couldn't have kids of their own, so they chose me. Mom used to tell me about it from as far back as I can remember. She often described how they went to the hospital in North Sydney and there I was—just eight days old—and she always said that the minute she laid eyes on me she knew I was...I was...destined to be her little girl."

Suddenly a tear ran down Jackie's cheek. She wiped it away and got up to find a tissue.

"Forgive me," she said as she blew her nose. "It's just that it's a bit rough right now. Dad died three years ago and now that Mom has Alzheimer's...she isn't her real self." Her voice trailed off into some far-away, sad place in her personal history.

"I'm really sorry, Jackie," consoled Andrea.

Jackie regained her composure. "So how did you hear this? Not that it's a secret. I suppose Aunt Roberta told you, did she?"

"No, she never talks to us much."

Jackie shook her head. "Poor old Roberta. She never

was very friendly."

"There's something else, now that I know your full name…" Andrea ventured.

"And what's that?"

"I know that you applied to find your birth mother."

Jackie's expression changed abruptly, her eyes narrowing. "How did you…? The only person who knows that is Steve. You surely didn't talk to him. He's been away all summer. Who…?"

Andrea could feel her heart pounding again. She felt as if she was losing her voice. She cleared her throat and began. "The reason I know about your search for your real mother…is…because your mother and my mother are…is…the same person."

Jackie stared at her in wide-eyed disbelief.

"Honestly! I'm not making this up. I only found out about it today. From my mom."

"Your mother is my mother?" gasped an incredulous Jackie.

"That's it," Andrea confirmed.

Jackie stared at Andrea hard for a few seconds, and it seemed as if she was going to start laughing again. Then she started shaking with sobs, and tears began rolling down her face. Suddenly Andrea wished she hadn't told her. Maybe someone from the agency should have written her a letter. Perhaps this kind of information was too overwhelming for anyone to cope with face to face. However, Jackie quickly regained her composure and spoke almost in her normal voice.

"Where is she? I want to see her."

Andrea got to her feet, shaking with relief. "She's sitting on your front steps. Can I invite her in?"

CHAPTER SEVENTEEN ❧

At first none of them knew what to say. These three
women, who all had eyes the same shade of blue, and
various shades of brown hair, could only smile at one
another and go through the motions of perfunctory
hugs. The mother of both Jackie and Andrea was the first
to speak.

"I'm Doris. Doris Marie Goodyear Baxter Osborne,"
she announced, reciting her given names, her maiden
name, the name of her dead husband, and the name of
her living husband. Andrea had never heard her mother
introduce herself that way to anyone before. Couldn't
she simply have said, "Hello, I'm your mother," or
something like that?

"I'm Jackie…" Jackie began, and then lost her voice
and couldn't finish saying her own name.

"You're Eleanor Jacqueline. I've wanted to meet you
again, well, all of your life and a big chunk of mine. I
didn't know your name until a few months ago. I can't
tell you what it means to me that I've found…" Then
she lost it. She couldn't finish the sentence as tears
began to stream down her face. Andrea hunted through
her pockets for a tissue but didn't find one. This was

so unlike her mother, who had never been at a loss for words. Jackie got a box of tissues from the bathroom and handed it to the distraught woman who had not seen her since she had given her up twenty-six years earlier. Jackie looked shaken too. She hadn't had time to prepare for this. She had to wipe a tear from her eye too. That was when Andrea noticed how much Jackie's eyes and eyebrows resembled those of her mother. Maybe that was why she had warmed to Jackie right from the start. There had been something familiar about her expression, something reassuring about her attitude, characteristics she couldn't have identified until this very moment.

Jackie finally managed to say, "Why don't I put the kettle on, and we'll have a cup of tea?"

"That would be l-lovely, th-thanks," stuttered Doris in a weak, little voice that Andrea wasn't accustomed to hear coming from her in-charge mother, a woman who had been a level-headed schoolteacher for many years.

"Andrea, you could take your mother…ah, Doris… um, our mother…" suggested Jackie, who didn't quite know how to address her newfound parent, "down the hall and have a look in at Kenzie. He's asleep now, but when he wakes up in the morning I'll tell him his new grandmother came to see him."

Andrea was jolted again. It hadn't crossed her mind until that very moment that her own mother was somebody's grandmother. Grandmothers were old. Her mother was far too young for this.

The prospect of seeing her grandson improved Doris's composure. She stopped crying and blew her nose. She walked down the hall with Andrea to stand in the doorway of Kenzie's bedroom. The little boy was sleeping soundly beside his teddy bear. Doris didn't say a word; she just fixed her gaze on his face. Andrea wanted to say, "Wait till you see him when he's wide awake. He's not the little angel he looks right now." But she said nothing. There would be plenty of time for her mother to get acquainted when Kenzie was awake the next day. And the next. And the next. Jackie and Kenzie were family now. From now on they would be part of one another's lives.

Andrea, Jackie, and Doris sat down around the kitchen table, glancing uneasily at one another. Jackie, who had not been expecting company, apologized that all she had to offer were store-bought cookies kept in the cupboard for Kenzie. Nobody cared.

At first it was not easy for Jackie and Doris to talk to each other, so Andrea, the one person they had in common, became the focus of their conversation. Jackie began describing what a fine young person Andrea was and how she put such energy into her summer job and how well she had accepted the challenge of acting in the film. Andrea squirmed. This sounded too much like a school report. The phone in the hall rang, and Jackie went to answer it.

"Hi, darling," they heard her say. It was her husband

calling from some distant place in Labrador. Steve seemed to be doing most of the talking because all they heard from Jackie was an occasional "Sure…great…mm hmm…okay." Then, "Steve, honey, I'd better go," they heard. "You see…my mother's here." There was a pause. "No, not Mom. My birth mother." There was another pause while Steve, who must have been as astonished as Jackie had been, tried to digest this startling news. "I'll tell you all about it when you get home. Lots of love, hon. Bye now.

"That was Steve," Jackie explained unnecessarily as she returned to the kitchen. "And guess what? He figures he'll be home in a couple of weeks. Winter comes early in northern Labrador and the job he's on is gearing down for the season, so his work is nearly over. He's a helicopter pilot, working with a team of geologists."

Andrea hadn't thought about Steve at all. She knew he existed, but Steve was just a name and a face in photographs in Jackie's house. An absent husband. Now, abruptly, he had become a relative, some kind of brother-in-law.

Jackie sat down and sipped her tea, looking very serious. "There's one thing we haven't mentioned," she said quietly. "Who was my father?"

There seemed to be no end to revelations on this extraordinary day. Andrea didn't really want to hear any more. She didn't want to think about whoever he was, the man who had been her mother's long-ago boyfriend. But she realized Jackie had a right to know.

Doris pulled herself up in her chair, cleared her throat, and spoke in a small but calm voice. "He came from Quebec, Jackie. He was third mate on a ship bringing iron ore from Sept-Îsles to Sydney. I met him at a dance in a union hall. After that we went out on dates whenever his ship was in port." She hesitated.

"Go on," urged Jackie, eager for more information.

"Well, there isn't a lot to tell, except that I thought I was in love…at the time. It turned out neither of us were. After a while he quit his lob on the ship, and he never came back to Sydney. He had often talked about moving to Montreal. I guess he did. I suppose I could have written to him, tried to find him somehow, but I… well, I didn't. He never knew about you."

Jackie didn't say anything for quite a while. Neither did Andrea. She sat there trying to imagine her mother's terrible situation all those years ago. What must it have been like, finding herself pregnant and having her boyfriend sail away and never return?

"What was his name?" asked Jackie.

"Pierre Bélanger."

"Bélanger," pronounced Jackie slowly. "Bélanger," she repeated. Then her expression brightened. "So it turns out I'm actually French after all. Wait till I tell Steve!"

"Only half French," noted Doris with a cautious little smile. "The other half comes from Newfoundland."

"Maybe I'll find him someday," mused Jackie.

"Maybe so," said Doris sadly. "But I was in Montreal

on a holiday once and I looked in the phone book and, well, you can't imagine how many people there are named Bélanger in Montreal."

"I suppose it's like all the MacDonalds in the Cape Breton phone book."

"Yes. So you'll probably have to settle for just me. And Andrea."

Jackie stood up, came around the table, and gave them each a kiss.

"You'll do." She smiled. "You'll do just fine."

CHAPTER EIGHTEEN ❧

RR1, Trillium Woods
Ontario L1A 0X0

Dear Jackie,

Mom and Brad and I are really happy that you and
Kenzie and Steve are coming here to spend Christmas
with us. I thought I'd drop you a line to bring you up to
date on everything.

As you know, I went home with Justine for a few
days when our jobs were over. I had a fabulous time!
I learned lots of things, like how to milk a cow, how
to collect eggs, what you feed to a pig (anything at all,
they're not fussy).

The last night I was there we had a bonfire on the
beach. Cory came all the way from Louisbourg to be
with Justine. It was Marc's idea for the four of us to have
a beach party before I had to go back to Ontario. Was
it ever romantic! There was a full moon that night. We
toasted marshmallows. We sang Cape Breton songs. Marc
told me he wanted me to come back next summer. I
told him I hoped I could. Sometimes I wish I could live
there.

When I got back to school in September, everybody wanted to know about my summer job and what it was like, etc., etc. Mrs. Greenberg (my history teacher) suggested I write an article about it and read it to the class. I described how the Fortress of Louisbourg got built the first time and then I explained how it came to be built the second time. I described my job and responsibilities. (I mentioned that I liked my boss!) Then I went on to tell about the film that was being made because I knew the kids would want to hear about that. At the end of the piece I said that the most wonderful thing happened to me in August when I learned that I wasn't an only child after all, and that I now had a sister.

Do you know what my teacher said when she heard that? She said, "Congratulations. I didn't know your mother had had a baby." Well, for a minute I couldn't stop laughing, and she gave me a strange look. It wasn't funny. It just sounded funny the way she said it. So finally I said that, yes, she did have a baby, but it was a long time ago. It was simply that I didn't meet her until last summer.

She still looked puzzled, so I told her the whole story. Well, not absolutely everything because that would take too long. She told me that this was a special experience, and she was glad I wanted to share it with others. And you know what? It turns out I'm not the only person who found out they had an unknown brother or sister. Two other kids came up and told me their stories of how their families were reunited. We are planning to form a club called the Secret Sibling Society. We're including you as a member. What do you think of that?

Love from your sister,
Andrea

ACKNOWLEDGEMENTS ❧

I am grateful to Anne O'Neill and to Roseanne Poirier
of the Fortress of Louisbourg, who led me behind the
scenes where I learned so much; to RCMP Corporal
Dave Tricket, who explained how police procedures
work; to Mary Elliott, for her tireless attention to detail
and her sage advice; to Robin Long, who provided
me with a place to work; and to Farley, who, as always,
encouraged me.